THE HAUNTED STREETS

THE VACANT EXORDIUM
BOOK 1

WYATT HAMBY

The Haunted Streets

Published by Digital Pulps, Houston, Texas
Hamby, Wyatt, 2016 – The Haunted Streets
ISBN: 978-0692924549
10 9 8 7 6 5 4 3 2
1. Mystery & Detective 2. Action & Adventure
Originally Published in April 2016
Second Printing – July 2017

WYATTHAMBY.COM

Being deeply loved by someone gives you strength,
while loving someone deeply gives you courage.

- Lao Tzu

ONE

Saturday, April 10, 1937.

THE POUNDING ON THE DOOR sounded like the police. He likely could have slept through the unrelenting intent of a hammering fist, but it was the dull hum of reverberating windows that roused him from a dream of fortunate encounters with remarkable women and even greater fortune at the card table.

Even with a face he thought he saw somewhere before, but just couldn't remember, a dream-inspired lady friend was still preferable to waking up and seeing that over-exuberant rookie wearing the constant wide-eyed naiveté of youth untested.

That must be why they call them dream girls.

The knocking continued, and Frank Palmer tore the blankets from his large frame and cast his legs over the side of the bed. Rubbing the slumber from his eyes, he stepped into his slippers and willed them toward the front door. Taking a detour along the way, he placed coffee on the stove to boil and lit a cigarette before continuing his sleepy sojourn.

As Palmer was reaching for the doorknob, the annoyance persisted, inciting what would have typically manifested as a voice of consternation that he was just not awake enough to summon. Clutching the handle, Palmer used his momentum of turning away from it to open the door without even bothering to see who it was.

"Thank God. We've been trying to reach you for the last hour. The operator says your phone is—"

Charlie Callaghan was drenched from head to toe. Practically everything he was wearing stuck to his lean, athletic frame, and even the starch was gone from his hat, which now faced overbearing integrity issues around the edges. Underneath the dripping brim, his brown hair was matted to his forehead, and he looked up both questioningly and expectantly to the larger man walking away.

Palmer waved a hand in the general direction of the telephone. "It's out of order."

The phone line hung lifelessly in a loose coil on the floor, completely detached from the wall. Callaghan redirected his attention when the voice called from the other room, "Coffee?"

"Sure." Callaghan shifted from one foot to the other, uninterested in standing in the doorway any longer in his current state of affairs.

Shedding his coat, he hung it on the rack just inside the door, frowning and half shaking his head in response to the rippling puddle that began to form around the base of the stand. Clear rivulets cascading from the brim of his fedora reminded him to temporarily part ways with it as well.

"Black's all I got."

"Black is fine."

Callaghan had never been to Palmer's house before. There was one instance where he waited on the front porch, but it was the first time he had actually stepped foot inside.

The house was orderly and organized, but the thing that was immediately noticeable was the lack of decoration, which made it conspicuous by absence. There were no paintings, no vases to hold flowers—not even so much as a photo on an end table. Callaghan thought the place would look a lot better with a woman's touch.

Palmer retrieved the kettle from the stove and poured the steaming contents into two mugs. One was nondescript white porcelain that he nodded his head toward as Callaghan reached out for it. The other black and looked as if it had been pieced together from fragments, cracks running through nearly every aspect of its form, with white areas indicative of chips that had never been found.

"You don't have an umbrella?"

"Busted my hump to get here after they woke me up. Then ran to the car, and it wasn't raining that hard at the time," Callaghan said, wrapping his hands around the mug to warm them.

"And I swear," Callaghan shook his head, "The quieter I try to be, the more noise I make. Knocked the clock over and woke up the wife again."

It was a fanciful wedding near the final days of fall. Palmer couldn't remember her name at the moment, though he didn't make an exorbitant effort to rack his brain. Gail. Geraldine. Something like that.

Her family was kind of well-to-do and went to extravagant means to make sure their daughter had the type of wedding befitting a Capulet bereft of tragedy. At first, they expressed concerns over their daughter marrying a cop, but once Callaghan had made detective, right before Christmas, their agitation subsided, knowing there was less of a chance their daughter would wake up and find herself a widow. At least, that was what Palmer had deduced from the situation.

The married couple didn't immediately go on their honeymoon. As busy as things had been in his career at the time, they instead had waited until after the first of the new year, at which point Callaghan was officially paired up with Palmer.

Callaghan wouldn't have been his first choice as a new partner. That position would have gone to Walter Graham—an experienced detective around Palmer's age whose partner had also recently retired. But it wasn't within Palmer's realm of authority to have the final decision on those types of matters.

And Callaghan was his third partner in as many years.

Palmer sat his empty mug in the sink with sentiment as if nestling a baby into a crib, "What time is it?"

"About three-thirty or so."

"I'm going to get dressed. Just put your mug in the sink when you're finished."

Callaghan was assigned as Palmer's partner four weeks ago, but he'd already learned the hard way, in that small amount of time, that his new partner wasn't much of a talker in the early morning—or what he'd called the last gasps of nightfall if you asked him. In fact, Callaghan had learned that Palmer wasn't one to be particularly verbose at all. Complex questions had thus far been met with simple answers, in most circumstances.

As Palmer entered the bedroom, Callaghan finally called out from the kitchen, "It's Morgan Maxwell."

"Morgan Maxwell? The radio guy?" Palmer splashed his face with cold water and looked up and into tired, deep blue eyes that had gradually become familiar. The fire had remained untended for the past few years and the only flicker that was left threatened to burn out at any given time. Wetting his hands again, he combed his dark hair back so that it looked even and halfway presentable. He figured he could forgo a shave this morning.

"Yeah, him. Showtime Theatre."

Palmer pulled his suspenders over his shoulders, "That's why you're beating the hell out of my door at three o'clock in the morning? He's dead?"

"From what they told me, shot in his study. After what looks like one heck of a struggle."

Callaghan finished his coffee and followed the instructions as to what to do with the mug, twisting the faucet to rinse it before leaving it alongside its fractured partner. "What I don't get," Callaghan called out, "A famous guy like that? It's going to be in the papers for weeks. There's no way the shooter could have gotten away and kept this quiet without drawing all kinds of heat and unwanted attention on himself."

Finally, Palmer settled *Maurice* into the holster snugly secured beneath one of his broad shoulders. Maurice was a .38 caliber Colt Detective Special, bathed in sleek black with a round butt grip frame that made it more comfortable for a warm palm with a cool trigger finger to be molded around the grip. The short barrel made the pistol easier to conceal and had gathered speed in becoming standard issue over the course of the past couple years.

Emerging from the bedroom, Palmer gave the kitchen a once-over, making sure he didn't leave anything burning and that all affairs were in order. "That's the thing, Callaghan. Lots of reasons people kill."

He led Callaghan to the coat rack, stretching his own black coat over his broad form and retrieving his hat from the top, "In our business, a lot of the time, you'll find out it's over money. Others, it's because of something unimportant or stupid, like jealousy or a perceived display of disrespect. Usually, these stiffs probably didn't merit a plot in God's Acre, but a lot of people do a lot of bad things. And sometimes when they do... Well, I guess they get what's coming to them."

Callaghan hadn't expected his external attire would have had time to dry within the few minutes he had been there, so he put his soggy fedora back atop his head devoid of preferable expectations, "I guess we're going to find out which of those Maxwell was."

* * * * *

"I can't believe you have a radio in your car. That's aces," Callaghan mused, half snickering with enthusiasm as they pulled out of Palmer's driveway.

For the past couple years, Palmer had noticed a sharp diminishment in his vision when it came to driving in the dark, so it made more sense to have Callaghan drive, even though they were in Palmer's car. If anything, it probably ensured a much safer journey.

"I kept a pretty well-off attorney from being on the business end of a disgruntled client's wrath."

Palmer inspected the interior of the car, even looking in the back seat, as if it were somehow unfamiliar to him, "So he gave me the car. Just wouldn't take no for an answer. The Motorola was already in it when he gave it to me."

He worked the dial, sifting through static and the hum of negative signals before finally settling when a voice that was mostly crisp presented itself to the two-man audience.

"—*early this morning, when Salvadore Barone passed away in his sleep. Mr. Barone was seventy-two years of age and is survived by two daughters, Sylvia and Martine, who were both reported to be present at the moment of his passing. Mr. Barone had long denied allegations pertaining to his involvement in organized crime, and no evidence had ever been produced that could factually implicate Mr. Barone. Although he was better known for that perhaps exaggerated legacy, Mr. Barone, more importantly, owned several factories within the city, where he provided gainful employment in these tough times and was respected in the community for his many charity contributions. We will try to get a statement later today from—"*

Palmer cut his eyes toward Callaghan.

"What?" Callaghan turned to look at Palmer for a moment before affixing his eyes back on the road. "Mob boss—excuse me, alleged mob boss—dies in his sleep. After all, the man was ancient. They say he outlived two different wives. Doesn't sound like there's any sign of foul play involved to me."

Salvadore Barone might as well have been king.

Immigrating to the States in the late 1800s when he was in his teens, Barone had taken small jobs here and there, running errands and sending telegraph messages. Eventually, he worked his way into the inner circle of the Ariosto Family, where his determination to push any obstacles out of the way brought him to the top, lining his pockets—much of which he spent on gold rings, something he had a penchant for.

In 1901, a bloody war between the Ariosto Family and their primary rival, the Cacciatore Consortium, left anyone with any prestige or influence dead in a variety of inconvenient locales. As one of the survivors, Salvadore Barone had no better opportunity to make his move. Assembling the shambles of each of the families, Barone rid the organizations of any loose ends and loose lips and brought them together under the same banner. The group went through a few different names before the obvious was finally settled upon, and the Barone Family came to fruition in 1904.

Following those events, any up and coming would-be businessmen who wanted to initiate operations in the city had to pay homage to Barone. It wasn't something they were forced to do at gunpoint, but it would almost assuredly be the point of a gun they found themselves facing if they somehow had a lapse of better judgment and a greater error of wisdom in their decision making.

Palmer was silent for a moment, tipping his hat low in the front and peering out the window, gazing at nothing in particular as the buildings, parked cars and fire hydrants crawled by like cut-outs on a movie set.

Callaghan glanced over as he took a turn, entering the main highway, and repeated himself, "What?"

"It's going to be open season now. Crocetti, Casadonte—all the small fish too—they're going to tear this place apart fighting over what's left."

After his first wife had passed away, Salvadore Barone married the older sister of Nicodemus Crocetti. Crocetti had been steadily coming up within their convoluted world of shallow truths and obligatory respect, always one hand reaching out for a shake and a goodwill gesture while a knife slumbered uneasily in the other. This was perhaps his best way into the circle, and he spared no effort and expense in ushering his sister to proceed with the arrangement.

"How do you know so much about all this?" Callaghan asked.

Palmer shrugged, "Been doing this a long time. I almost had a case against Barone a couple years ago, but some of the evidence went for a walk and never came back. After that, everything fell through."

The outset of the early morning sky yawned, and several sprinkles peppered the windshield as Callaghan pulled off the freeway and into a residential area on the outskirts of the city. "Why did you become a cop?"

"I don't think we've been on enough dates to be getting all sweet and personal. You don't even call me by my first name yet. And I sure don't remember you buying me dinner."

Callaghan sighed. He could never quite tell when Palmer was speaking in jest. In either case, his new partner always wore the same sardonic expression, whether he just wanted to be left alone or was trying to goad a suspect into taking a swing at him. His understanding over recent weeks was that Palmer wasn't one for conversation to begin with—either that or he just didn't like him.

"To catch bad guys," Palmer finally answered.

It wasn't the insightful expression of worldly wisdom Callaghan was looking for, but he let it rest at that.

TWO

THE ASHES DARKENED in the air before they were taken by the night, and Milford Burrows exhaled cigarette smoke into the wind.

The sound of droplets shaken every so often from spring's early morning leaves—residue from the night's rain—was his only fickle companionship as he stood the past two hours a lone sentinel on a dead man's front porch.

The house was even more impressive on the inside than it was without. A spacious two-story affair with at least five bedrooms, as best Burrows could tell from the limited minutes he was inside, though one of them possibly could have been converted into a study at some point.

Burrows cursed underneath his breath and invoked his religion as another set of headlights appeared in the driveway. It was sure to be them this time. The vultures had a habit of showing up before the body even got cold. Almost two months on the job and Burrows hadn't even caught a criminal yet. All he had done so far was stand in front of houses testing the limits of his anxiety as he made his best effort of parrying questions until someone could come out and provide some real answers.

As real as those answers got, anyway.

Two car doors slammed, and Burrows narrowed his eyes as a pair of figures in plain clothes approached the front porch.

"Relax, Mill, it's just us." The voice made Burrows finally distribute his weight evenly on both feet.

"Charlie? Thank God." Burrows reached out for a handshake as Callaghan and Palmer entered the luminosity cast by the front porch light and ascended the steps.

Palmer looked around, "Who else we expecting?"

"Reporters."

"Still too early for all that. You can bet they'll be riding in on the back of the sun, though," Palmer said.

"Wonderful. The Captain's here," Burrows pointed out, nodding to the assortment of cars parked sporadically in the driveway.

"Yeah, we saw his car," Callaghan said. "Any particular reason he's here?"

"Mr. Radio Big Shot, Morgan Millions, I gather," Burrows shrugged, peering between the two detectives and into the distance, "Is that a thirty-four Buick? Jeez Charlie, was that a wedding present?"

"Actually, it's his," Charlie said.

"Detective must be a hell of a pay raise," Burrows remarked.

They always have something to say about the car.

There were probably rumors floating around that Palmer could have been on the take, but no one of any importance would have believed such a thing. He knew the car might draw that sort of questioning, which was why he had refused the gift several times before finally agreeing just for the sake of ending the conversation.

Over ten years on the job and Palmer had only exhibited questionable behavior in the form of being a little too rough with suspects on occasion. The thoughts and hushed whispers of those who didn't know any better were of no consequence to him.

Palmer's response was not of a vocal nature, grasping the door handle to signify the end of the conversation.

"I guess it's time to see if we can figure out why bullets killed the radio star," Charlie said, patting Burrows on the shoulder. "Take care, Mill. We'll catch up later."

Burrows twisted toward them as the two men went inside, "It's upstairs—second door on the—"

Palmer closed the door harder than was necessary.

* * * * *

A flashbulb lit the wall outside the study with a momentary rectangle of white, signifying the location in which the departed Morgan Maxwell was to be discovered.

Palmer and Callaghan emerged from the hallway to find four others in plain clothes, and an equal number of uniforms.

"Hey, look—there he is—Mr. Semi-Newlywed." Lewis Murray, one of the uniforms—and the one with the camera—announced the arrival of the pair, causing everyone else to turn toward the doorway. "How was the honeymoon, Charlie?"

Murray was Callaghan's former partner. They had ridden the streets together for five years before Charlie's promotion.

"It was swell. And nice to take a little breather before getting back to business. We went to Vegas."

"Well, at least that was after you were married. How's Geneva?" Murray approached to shake hands. "She adjusting to the married life?"

Callaghan shook his head, "She might be if I'd quit waking her up every morning."

Palmer and Callaghan fanned out across the room, with the former approaching one of the men in plain clothes. "Captain."

"Good to see you, Frank."

In the annals of police history, John Benjamin was somewhat of a local folk legend—an eternally unruffled mountain of grit, even larger than Palmer. Although he was climbing the rungs of age's ladder, there was no frailty in the dignity and rigidity in which Benjamin carried himself. He had been a combat pilot during the war, and the fact that he shot down nearly twenty German planes was something that was commonly known, yet knowledge he held in modesty and reservation whenever it came up for discussion. Benjamin had survived the war, survived the aftermath that came with it and survived the streets during prohibition. And he hadn't even so much as stumbled along the way. The modern world held no more proving grounds for him.

"What have we got so far, John?" Palmer joined Benjamin in regarding the man on the floor.

Morgan Maxwell was still in his suit and tie, sprawled out in the middle of the study like a centerpiece decorating the room as if intended to be the center of attention that he was in life. What remained of polished brass and shards of glass mixed with a short crimson tributary looked like it could have once been a table now crushed beneath his spiritless weight.

"I just got here, myself." Benjamin gestured toward Maxwell, "You know, I've never seen what he looks like. Just heard his voice. He looks different from what I always pictured, though. Kind of a weasely little guy..."

Benjamin moved forward with the scarce details he knew at this point, "Anyway. Hit twice, it looks like. One in the neck and one in the chest. Both from the front. No murder weapon, so far, of course."

"Of course." Palmer stepped over the blood to get a closer look at Maxwell from the front, "Any chance we found some casings?"

Joe McCreary took a drag of his cigarette and piped up, "No. Might have been a revolver."

His partner, Jesse Fisher chimed in, "Yeah, either that or the shooter picked them up before he left."

Palmer was musing aloud as much as he was responding to Fisher, "A fight and gunshots heard by the neighbors—anyone talk to them yet?"

The fourth of the plain clothes men already on the scene when Palmer and Callaghan arrived said, "I'm about to go door-to-door now."

Walter Graham had been doing this almost as long as Palmer. They were nearly paired up as partners a few months back, but Palmer ended up with Callaghan instead.

"The ones immediately next door called it in, so I told them I'd give them time to get dressed and get their wits about them before I came back. Which it's about time to do." Graham instructed one of the uniforms to go with him before he made his departure from the study.

"There was no forced entry on the front door. How about the others?" Palmer asked.

McCreary shrugged, "Everything else is still in order. Doors. Windows, too."

As he stood from the crouching position he took to survey Maxwell, Palmer asked, "What else we got, then?"

"Two ledger books," Fisher answered, "On the desk there. We pulled them off the bookcase. One is recent, and the other is from thirty-five."

"No thirty-six?"

"Not on this shelf, anyway."

Palmer adjusted his hat as he approached the desk.

He paused for a moment to observe a pair of contraptions astride a long table against the west wall. A phonograph of a few years in age sat contiguous to a boxy black machine that Palmer could only guess was a record lathe of some sort, especially since it was connected to an RCA 44A microphone that would never again capture the jovial sounds of the familiar radio voice. The cost of the lathe and microphone alone would have been stiff. Ordinary people couldn't be disposed to these types of luxuries. Running his hand atop the gleaming brass horn of the phonograph as he walked away, Palmer's momentary distraction was abolished when he recalled the ledger books.

Bound in quality leather, one of the books had the typical brown coloring one might expect, and the other was a deeper reddish-brown combination that reminded him of clay typically found in the southeastern part of the country.

"You go through them yet?" He asked.

Palmer glanced over to Callaghan, who had been walking around the study and seemed to be examining everything. He pulled the cushions from the sofa and returned them exactly as they had been. He inspected the large set of double windows and even looked behind the drapes before perusing the bookcase they had been referring to.

"I flipped through them a little," McCreary answered in Fisher's stead. "But they don't make any sense."

"What do you mean?" Palmer picked up the brown one, opening it to a random page in the first quarter of the ledger, noting that it was the one from this year.

"The entries don't denote whether the money is going out or coming in. It's just lumped all together like a grocery list."

Scanning the page he was on, Palmer reached an immediate conclusion, "They're done that way so that only Maxwell could tell which was which. The real details are—were—in his head."

"Plus," Fisher said, "None of the names are actually names. Just 'Mr. C.' and such..."

Everyone in the room knew the reason for that was because Maxwell didn't want anyone else knowing who the names really were, should they happen to find the ledger books. It didn't take a detective to point that out.

Palmer rummaged through the pages, looking specifically for the entries that included the aforementioned Mr. C. There were at least two of these on every page, and in each instance, the numbers were either very high or minuscule.

"I think it's debt," Palmer surmised.

"What?" McCreary and Fisher came over to have a look, and Palmer placed the open ledger back on the desk so they could see for themselves.

"Look," Palmer pointed, "One thousand fifty dollars here. Then, down here, one hundred twenty-five dollars. The big number is what he owes; small number is what he's paying back."

"But see, they don't add up—subtract—whatever, you know what I mean," Fisher said.

"That's because here—in the middle—three hundred thirty, which is going to add to the total owed." Palmer flipped to the next page, "Which he never totals on the same page as the additions."

Palmer inspected the numbers more carefully on the next page, "Damn, that's peculiar..."

"How's that?" McCreary asked.

"The big number never gets any smaller. It's like he's in a hole and he just keeps digging."

* * * * *

Benjamin approached Callaghan while he was inspecting the bookcase. "It was a nice wedding, Charlie."

"Thank you, Captain. I'm glad you could make it. Geneva said it was a pleasure to finally meet you, after hearing so much about the people I work with."

"Speaking of which, how are things with your new partner?"

"I don't think he likes me. He's just so—was he like this when you two were partners?"

Benjamin put his hands in his coat pockets, "I know. Frank has all the charm of a lump of coal. But trust me, he'll warm up once you've been in the fire with him."

"He doesn't want to talk about anything, really. Anytime I ask him a question—trying to get to know him better—it seems like I'm testing his nerves, so I just let it die. I feel like I do all the talking most of the time. Even if you've got a keen eye for detail and decent deductive reasoning skills, he's hard to read, you know?"

"I'll drop you a bone, then. What do you want to know?"

"Do you happen to know why he calls his gun Maurice?"

Benjamin failed to stifle a chuckle, "Of all the things to ask..."

"Why? Is it a sore subject?"

"No, not that. But sure, I told you I'd give you one."

Benjamin turned to look at Palmer, who was still going through the ledger books with McCreary and Fisher.

The Captain's voice lowered, "It was his second week on the force. Frank was the first to arrive at a house fire. He kicked the front door open and went inside. By this time, it had been burning for awhile, and most of the walls and ceiling were already ablaze. He called out, but got no answer, so he went upstairs to see if the rest of the house was clear."

Benjamin glanced over his shoulder again to assure Frank was still occupied. Then, he turned back to Charlie, "Let's go over here. "

The two approached the window, on the opposite side of the room from the topic of their discussion.

"The downstairs was clear, but when he made it upstairs, he heard someone crying. But the fire stood between the stairs and any of the rooms up there. So he takes off his coat and belt, wraps the coat around the belt, and uses it to bat at the fire, trying to stifle it so he could move through."

"He found them?" Charlie asked of the crier.

"In one of the back bedrooms. It was an older kid— maybe ten or so—the parents had left alone. I think they were out at dinner if I remember it right."

Benjamin could see all the cars parked outside. They weren't in any kind of order whatsoever, and the only thing anyone looking at them from the second floor could tell from their disheveled arrangement was the likelihood of which cars had arrived first.

"That was fast," Benjamin said. "I'm going to assume we won't have any witnesses, either."

It took Charlie a moment to figure out what he was referring to, but then he noticed Graham and the uniform below, walking back from the house next door.

"Anyway. We'll deal with that when Graham gets back up here." Benjamin continued, "So Frank doesn't let that door stop him either, and he goes in and grabs the kid. I think it was a little girl. He scoops her up and heads back to the stairs, and she's crying and kicking, but he can't figure out what it is. Frank tries to assure her things are okay and that he's getting her to safety, but she keeps kicking the hell out of his shins like she doesn't want to go. And he notices the door to the water closet is closed."

"There was someone else?" Callaghan interjected.

Benjamin held up a hand to stave off further questions as the corner of his wide jaw curled.

"Well, that's about the minute I pull up. I'm just in time to see this rookie Palmer come running out the door of this mansion ablaze—kid in one arm and dog in the other."

He didn't attempt to suppress the chuckle this time. "It was a picture perfect moment, too, but the press wasn't there yet, so they missed their chance."

He had always figured Palmer was probably thankful for that.

The Captain's flippancy was as quiet as he was able to force it as he shook his head, "Damndest thing I ever saw."

"I think they finally determined the fire was caused by an electrical problem. But, as a gesture for saving their little girl's life, the family gave Palmer the dog."

Charlie grinned as he reached his own conclusion, "And the dog's name was Maurice..."

"I swear, I think Frank had that dog about ten years."

"It's hard to believe Palmer had a man's best friend. A best friend of any kind, really. It must have been pretty stout."

Benjamin's face became one of mock seriousness as he raised his eyebrows high, "Fiercest Pembroke Welsh Corgi you ever saw. Seriously, though, every time I went to his house, that dog bit the back of my heels."

The Captain's expression changed, and Callaghan had the distinct impression he was having a battle internally, but then decided to go ahead.

"To be honest, I thought you were going to ask about Mortuary."

Callaghan's interest piqued. "The place where people are buried? Or that silly thing the papers keep talking about?"

"Guy in the papers."

As the stories went, "Mortuary" was the imposing moniker the city newspapers—most notably *The Amendment*—had seen fit to bestow upon a supposed man dressed in black that had been seen by several unreliable witnesses over the past few months and was believed to be responsible for the deaths of a handful of proven criminals. Callaghan was of the majority who put no stock in the stories.

"I can't really bring myself to believe anything *The Amendment* writes anymore," Charlie said. "It's like they make up news, just trying to sell papers. In thirty-three, they ran that story where a reporter claims to have practically chased Nick Chopper through the forest. There was never any proof or follow-up to the story, naturally."

"Who?" The Captain shrugged, and Charlie realized that he was only half paying attention.

"I don't really mean him, but—you know, Nick Chopper—the Tin Woodman." Charlie recalled the story fondly. It had always been one of his favorites. "He made a living chopping down trees until a witch put a curse on his axe and it chopped off his limbs, one by one. Every time he lost one, the limb was replaced with one made of tin, until there was nothing left of Nick Chopper but parts created from tin. The tinsmith who helped him forgot to replace his heart, and he was no longer able to love his sweetheart. "

Benjamin was nonplussed. "Charlie…"

"Never mind, it's from some books I read as a kid."

"This isn't a newspaper or a storybook, Charlie. Ask Palmer what he saw at Rohde Falls."

THREE

THE RED LEDGER BOOK felt lighter in Palmer's hand; perhaps not weighted as much by the guilt found within.

"Look at this," Palmer said to McCreary and Fisher, "Every third week of the month, there's the same amount listed to something called Season Heights."

Fisher nodded, "That's that upper crust digs over on Arbor."

In parenthesis, following the notation of the payment being made to the apartment building, there was a name listed as Miss F.

"Anyone know if Maxwell had a girl?" Palmer raised his voice, asking the room.

"Sure he did. There was that blonde—you know," Fisher looked at McCreary as he snapped his fingers, trying to come up with the name, "—the one who tried to be an actress, thinking Maxwell was going to take her with him to the stars."

"Roselyn Farrell," Callaghan called out. "She was in that picture *A Simple Moment*. I took my wife to see that one before we got married. We didn't think it was that bad, but I guess others—mostly the critics—disagreed with us. And that was pretty much the end of her car—"

Charlie was walking back from the windows, Benjamin behind him, when something caught his peripheral vision, eliciting an instinctual double-take. He pointed to the wooden panels beneath their feet.

"Bullet hole in the floor."

Everyone gathered around. The penetration was clean, directly between the parts where two of the varnished boards met, and was in a darker part of the wood, making it so the hole could only be seen if viewed from the window.

Palmer knelt down to examine the hole, then looked up to Callaghan. "Think you can get it out?"

"Probably a heck of a lot easier than whoever gets those two out of Maxwell later." Callaghan knelt down beside him, running his finger over the smooth aperture.

Callaghan's father had been a medic during the war and had gone on to become a surgeon of some renown. Palmer was aware of this fact, as Callaghan had recounted during their first day working together, and he hoped that meant that Callaghan would have the type of steady hands required to cause minimal damage to the slug when removing it from the floor boards.

Walter Graham returned to the study with the uniform in tow. He saw everyone else huddled around Charlie Callaghan, knife in hand, and went on to make his report to the Captain, "Neighbors heard the shots but didn't see anyone. That would be because they didn't even look outside. The husband locked the doors while the wife called us."

The others were probably listening, but no one looked up from the seemingly exclusive enclosure that currently warranted their attention.

"Got it," Callaghan professed as he opened his palm to reveal the bullet—almost entirely still intact. He closed his knife with the other hand, returning it to his coat pocket.

"I'm going to say that one looks like a .38 caliber," Benjamin said.

Taking a gander at the bullet in Callaghan's hand himself, Palmer had no reason to disagree. It had been his experience that Benjamin was always right when it came to accurately concluding the caliber of bullet in instances where the slug wasn't damaged too badly.

"Anything else?" Benjamin asked of the detectives.

Graham cleared his throat, "Yes, there's this, Captain." He produced a large black button from his pocket, handing it over to Benjamin.

"What's this?" Benjamin held the button aloft with two fingers, eyeing it closely. Inscribed in the material was a large letter B.

"It was near the window when we first got here," Fisher said, "And it doesn't go with anything in this room."

McCreary added, "Or with what Maxwell is wearing."

"That B—that's Bankston Brower. Those are not clothes the average guy can just get his hands on. If I had to guess, I'd say it's from a topcoat," Graham informed.

Palmer took another look around the study. "The killer may have already been here. Waiting for Maxwell."

"Go ahead, Frank," Benjamin said.

Palmer walked toward the window.

"No broken windows and none of the doors were kicked in. It's possible the shooter was already here, in Maxwell's study."

He turned around to face the other men, "He could have even been hiding behind these drapes, lying in wait in the dark. Maxwell comes in, turns on the lights, and then gets settled at his desk there. The killer emerges from behind the drapes, but Maxwell catches him. Maybe the intruder hesitates—maybe Maxwell is just that fast. They start to fight, and the gun goes off, making Callaghan's hole in the floor. The shooter knocks Maxwell back—could have even fallen and broken the table at that point. Then, when Maxwell gets up, he isn't fast enough this time to prevent the next two times the killer squeezes that iron."

Callaghan rounded out the theory, "Then, back into the glass—no more Morgan Maxwell. No casings to pick up, because it's a .38, and the killer gets away without being seen."

Benjamin nodded and started making assignments as he buttoned his coat.

"Okay, I want Palmer and Callaghan on this one. McCreary and Fisher will provide support if needed. I'm going to leave these uniforms to wait for the meat wagon to pick up Mr. Maxwell. They'll also assist in blocking off the scene and dealing with the buzzards when they get here. I'm going home to have a nightcap. Get some rest if you can. Callaghan, you have the magic eye tonight, so take the ledger books with you and go through them thoroughly in the morning. I'm going to keep a twenty-four-hour guard posted here for the next couple weeks. Lot of thieves in these times. And we don't need any evidence tainted in case we ever need to come back."

Palmer already knew what the Captain was going to say next. He hated being the bearer of bad news, especially when he knew he was going to have to stand there and watch an awkward waterworks show.

"Meanwhile, Palmer will be having a friendly discussion with Miss Farrell. And for the love of God,

Frank, please try to put your best empathy forward this time."

FOUR

Sunday, April 11, 1937.

IT WAS THE BEST DAY of George King's life. As the man getting off the elevator pressed a nickel into George's hand, he thanked him with a smile and closed the elevator cage door. George then threw the lever that was to return him to the bottom floor.

George had been the elevator attendant at Season Heights for nearly thirty years—since the first day the building went up in 1908—and he had always done no less than what was expected of him. Take a pleasant demeanor with the residents, be thankful of any gratuities doted upon him and throw the lever.

Having heard countless conversations between riders over the years, George did what he always did: he kept his head down, did the job he was paid to do and allowed rumors to travel from ear to ear and into thin air.

He wasn't sure how it started, but in recent years, several of the residents had begun referring to him as King George, ruler of the elevator.

His friendly personality and likable comportment had ensured that George remained employed for nearly three decades, and it offered him a vaccination against the depression—something most people had been susceptible to.

Even if the management changed their policy from week to week, George adjusted to their expectations. Sometimes the policy was to keep quiet and just run the elevator, so as to not bother the patrons. Sometimes the management said to be as friendly and talkative as possible.

Making friends, they called it.

George wasn't really sure which one it was this week, but he had decided from the moment the sun rose that today was going to be one of jubilance.

As the elevator touched the ground floor, George drew the cage to the side and waved an inviting arm, beckoning the tall gentleman in black to enter. The man's long coat was open, and the badge attached to his belt did not pass without notice.

"What floor, sir?" George asked.

"Eleventh."

"And how are you this beautiful morning, sir, if I may kindly petition? It's nice to see the rain has stopped."

Palmer refrained from speaking until he didn't have to do so over the sound of the elevator cage closing.

"I'm Good. Yourself?"

George put his lever arm to use, and the elevator initiated its ascent. "Oh, it's just the best day of my life, sir. Wrapping up thirty years on the job today."

"Retiring?"

"Well, Friday was really my last day, but the snapper I've been training to take my place had a death in the family, so I told them I'd work through the weekend before I finally get to have some quality time with the wife."

Palmer could only imagine the amount of training that went into closing a door and pulling a lever.

When he didn't answer, George asked, "What brings you to the fabulous Season Heights, detective?"

The elderly man was talkative, that was for sure, but he had a bespectacled face of pinkish colored cheeks that reminded Palmer of his great grandfather Elias—the type of face that could be trusted and meant no harm to anyone in the world.

He figured it was time to get the man discussing something of importance. Palmer pulled his coat closed, covering his badge.

"What do you know about Roselyn Farrell?"

"Miss Rose? Is she in some kind of trouble?"

"To be determined." Palmer asked again, "So, what do you know about her?"

"What I heard, she was an actress in Commiewood before moving out here. I didn't see the picture, myself. She's a lovely lady, though, if that's what you're asking."

"Has anyone visited her lately?"

George pushed his glasses high on his nose. "Sure. That same ole skinny fella brought her some flowers again not too long ago. I don't know his name, but every time I talk to him, I get the impression I've met him somewhere else before. And he's a good tipper, too."

Maxwell. It's the voice that makes him seem familiar.

"When was that?"

George paused for a moment as the elevator crawled to rest, having reached the eleventh floor. "This is your stop." Then, he answered the question, "Two weeks ago...maybe?"

As George opened the elevator door, Palmer asked, "What's the going rate?"

The elderly man turned, wrinkling his face more than usual, "Sir?"

"You said the man was a good tipper. I assume that's part of a subtle tactic to remind me that gratuities are appreciated."

"No sir, that's not what I meant at all. I was just— "

"How much?"

"Usually a nickel or a dime."

Frank produced a money clip and rolled a dollar from the middle. He folded it once and handed it to the elevator operator. "Here. Enjoy your retirement."

Thanking him heartily, George couldn't wipe the smile from his face. His mouth curled upward to meet the curves outside his eyes, reminiscent of a cartoon character. "And I'll still be here when you're ready to go back down, sir."

* * * * *

Roselyn Farrell's apartment was almost on the opposite side of the building from the elevator—apartment 1121.

By now, Callaghan was probably nose-deep in the ledger books. He had the easy job. But informing Miss Farrell about Maxwell's death was only a small part of the reason he was here.

The Captain had advised Palmer the night before that even if she didn't know the details of Maxwell's gambling dealings, the chances were good that she could have been there in at least one of the instances where he was racking it up.

The news was guaranteed to be in this morning's paper and was probably reported on the radio, too, if it hadn't been overshadowed so far by the coinciding death of Salvadore Barone last night. Maybe she already knew, and he wouldn't have to break it to her.

Taking a deep breath, Palmer knocked with purpose.

Hearing footfalls approach the door, he silently rehearsed his introduction—not because he had any reservations regarding the delivery of sorrowful words, but because he wanted to be able to perform his speech without thinking. He needed to observe her initial reaction while they were still unfamiliar.

Watch this one carefully. Remember, she was an actress.

As the door opened, Palmer began. "Good evening, Miss Farr—"

Frank nearly lost his words.

Standing before him in the doorway was a blonde in her early to mid-twenties, with her hair still in a fashionable up-do, pulled clear of her face so that it formed tight curls in the back. Her cheekbones were pronounced, sitting high on an angular and patrician face that had already been expertly made-up with dusky eyeshadow and deep red lips.

Still clothed in her white long-sleeved negligee—which was untied and completely open in the front—her ivory undergarments were on full display, wearing the newer briefs that were popular with the younger crowd, more contoured to the body and doing little to hide a curvaceous figure.

As a proper gentleman was wont to do, Palmer averted his gaze, but he knew it had lingered too long already. Eyes downcast, he noted that the burgundy rug in front of the door could use a good beating.

"Miss Farrell, your nightgown—"

"Yet only one of us seems to be embarrassed by it."

If she was going to try to throw him off by answering the door in her unmentionables, then two could play at that game.

Snatching his badge from his belt, Palmer almost stuffed it into the woman's face. The blonde had to draw her head back for her eyes to focus on it. Then, he lowered it to block the view, making it so that he had no choice but to keep his eyes above shoulder level.

If her present state had been intended to be a distraction, then it had lost its luster—it may as well have been a man standing there.

"Good morning, Miss Farrell. I'm detective Frank Palmer. I was hoping I could ask you a few questions."

"Yes, of course. Come inside."

The apartment was more spacious on the inside than it looked from the hallway. A black and gold Persian rug adorned the center of the main room, while there was a bar on the back wall. The windows probably offered a decent view of the city from this height, but the curtains were still drawn, allowing for scant natural lighting to enter.

Palmer removed his hat as Miss Farrell closed the door behind him. The apartment smelled of a woman living alone—a combination of honeysuckle and expensive perfume that was amiable to the senses.

The woman then passed him by and made her way to the bar, taking a bottle and placing it next to a glass that looked like it had already seen some use this morning.

"Brandy?"

Palmer shook his head. "No thanks—I don't drink much."

With her back to him, Miss Farrell pulled the silken belt of her gown, tying it snugly closed.

"You don't drink much, or you don't drink often?"

"Both," he said.

Miss Farrell shrugged, and opened the bottle anyway, pouring dark contents into the glass that was at the ready. She turned around, glass in hand. "So, what brings you here this morning, Detective?"

Frank had been inspecting the room. There were two paintings on different walls—he didn't know who the artist was. They didn't look like anything he remembered seeing in his history books in school.

When he turned to face the front door, he saw the room's main attraction—well, aside from the woman in it.

The movie poster on the wall had to be at least three feet in length and was encased in an ornate frame. A well-dressed man with a bowler hat he was raising just over his head wore a toothy grin as if he were in the middle of laughing. His other arm was wrapped around Roselyn

Farrell, stuffed into a tight-fitting red dress that buttoned along the front. Her hairstyle didn't look very different from its current state, even with that little red and white hat cocked sideways atop it.

The title of the picture was typed bold and clear at the top: *A Simple Moment.*

"What's it about?" Palmer pointed to the poster.

"Somehow, I'm not surprised you didn't see it." Miss Farrell joined his side, looking at the poster fondly.

As she approached, he noticed she was wearing white fitted slippers that reminded him of something a ballet dancer might wear. He had actually been dragged to the ballet once, but that seemed like a lifetime ago.

"It's about a traveling vaudevillian that finally gets his big break on stage and discovers his future co-star during a train ride. She has talent with her voice, but she can't dance a step, so he has to teach her after he talks the producer into giving her the part."

No wonder he didn't see it.

With her appearance now being that of someone presentable, Palmer was able to give her a look-over with minimal discomfort.

"No church this morning?"

She raised the glass of brandy, "I just haven't felt like getting dressed yet today, detective. Besides, I don't know if you're familiar, but it's considerable preparation for a lady to get ready to go out to meet the big, wide world.

You have to wear this, and you have to wear that—I should think it no surprise that a man invented these things."

Palmer shrugged, "Most things were invented by a man, so it shouldn't be a surprise at all. Besides, that man didn't put those things on, wear them around and make them fashionable, so I'd take that up with your fellow ladies if you have a complaint. I also doubt the inventor of the necktie bragged about comfort and practicality."

He didn't expect that she would find humor in his words, as that was not his intent, but delightful laughter erupted from the woman as she placed a hand on his shoulder, which he turned his eyes to until she removed it.

"You must keep your wife in stitches," she said.

That was not a direction Palmer was willing to take the conversation. "Have you seen the paper this morning?"

Miss Farrell turned away from him, raising a hand to her face. A lone sniffle was the only indication that she knew what he was referring to.

"Yes. It's on the front page of this morning's *Amendment*."

The front page? It seemed strange to Palmer that Maxwell would make the front page and not Salvadore Barone. Either Maxwell was more famous than he thought, or it was because Barone didn't get shot in his house.

With her back to him, Palmer made a fruitless attempt to analyze her tears, but when she whirled to face him again, twin streams of that dark eye shadow stained her cheeks.

If she were that good of an actress, she would have made more than one picture.

A small pang of guilt nagged at his conscience, and he realized he hadn't taken the Captain's advice regarding empathy.

"I apologize, Miss Farrell." He took the handkerchief from his coat pocket, offering it to the blonde.

"No, it's okay. I thought I had already done most of my grieving this morning. And please," she sniffed again, touching the cloth to her nose and then each cheek, "Call me Rose."

Giving her a moment to collect herself, Palmer waited for her to speak again. She clutched the handkerchief tightly, taking another drink of her brandy.

"Do you know who did it—who is responsible?"

"Not yet," Palmer said, shaking his head. "I was hoping you might have some insight. I have to ask: Did Maxwell have any enemies that you know of?"

Rose scoffed, "Only every wanna-be there ever was." Her tone changed from sorrow to one of bitterness. "Morgan grew up in a house with a dirt floor—scratching and clawing for every nickel he ever had. His father was in the war, and he was never the same after he came back.

Couldn't work. Couldn't hold down a job. Morgan had at least two jobs to support that family—including his mother and sister—I think he stopped attending school when he was fourteen. Then, he got his lucky break one day, appeared on the radio, and the rest is history, as they say."

Hanging on every word so far, Palmer considered placing his hat on the hook on the wall so that he'd stop idly fidgeting with it, but he didn't expect to be in her presence much longer.

"There are plenty of people in this world, Detective Palmer, who didn't put in half the time, half the work and half the effort to deserve what some people have. But their own rancor and lack of self-worth lead them to believe that those people don't deserve it either. Maybe looking for some of these failures will result in your success."

Rose also seemed as if she felt like she worked hard to get that movie role. Maybe she did. He shook his head, though. It was doubtful that some second-rate radio guy would kill Maxwell just so he could be number one.

"I have reason to believe Maxwell may have had some—dealings—possibly involving gambling and likely with the wrong people."

The blonde poured herself another drink, "The wrong people like Arturo Casadonte?"

Pulling that name from nowhere was as unexpected as brazenly saying it without looking over her shoulder.

"You know him?" Palmer asked.

"Sure," Rose said. "We met a few times. Morgan went to his clubs pretty regularly. After showing me off to everyone for awhile, he always ended up taking a private meeting with what he called some people."

"Did this happen often?"

Rose shrugged, "Oh, just about every club we ever went to."

The detective was listening for something specific—anything that could have possibly tied Maxwell's death to Casadonte.

"Did you ever see or overhear anything? Some of their dealings, maybe?"

"No," she said, peering into her glass as she lightly swirled it about. "I never went into any of the back rooms. His wife was really pleasant company to be around, though. Do you think the mob killed Morgan over some sort of debt?"

"I think it's starting to look that way," Palmer said. "Do you know anything about his bookkeeping? Notes, records he may have retained?"

"I know he was always scribbling in one of those books. He'd get pretty angry if you talked to him while he was trying to do the numbers."

Palmer nodded. "We found a few of them. My partner is going through those to see what we can find. Hopefully, something can be found in those that we can use."

"Is that how you got my address?" Rose asked.

"Yes," Palmer said. "Season Heights was one of the most common listings... As far as the larger numbers were concerned."

Rose furrowed her arched brows. "A little money certainly seems like an impulsive reason to risk going to prison for murder."

"Well," Palmer said as he returned his hat to the purpose it was made for, "It's one of the main reasons. Especially when it's not just a little."

Rose sat her glass on the bar, nodding.

He reached into his coat and produced a small card. "Here, take this. You can reach either me or my partner, Detective Callaghan, at this number and address."

Palmer hadn't noticed the snow globe on the mantle before, but it came into view over Rose's shoulder as she took the card from his hand. The Eiffel Tower stood within the glass sphere, a few white flakes stuck to some of the protrusions.

"Have you ever been to Paris?" Palmer asked.

Rose looked at the snow globe, assuming that was the reason he asked. "Yes. Morgan and I took a trip there when we were still together."

"Still together? Yeah, it's my understanding that the two of you were on the breaks."

"Our relationship was like the crashing of waves on the beach, detective. Sometimes full of vigor—other times pulled away by the tide."

Tears filled her eyes once more. She would never have the chance to repair things with him again—never receive the bouquet he always showed up with when it was time for the two of them to make up.

Palmer asked a question he already knew the answer to. "He kept up the payments on your apartment through the summer, right?"

"Yes," Rose nodded, momentarily bringing the handkerchief to her delicate nose once again. "He always took very good care of me."

What was it going to be like now? Maxwell was going to be memorialized by tomorrow, and her chance at show business had already expired. Palmer wondered if the reality of that had hit her yet, but it wasn't his place to say. If not, it would come in its own time.

"What's it like—Paris?" He asked. "They say it's the city of romance."

"Oh, it's not that at all." Rose chuckled. "The people are impertinent, wrapped up in their own fraudulent cultural superiority and the Bohemians that go there to languish uselessly in their liberal freedoms would never tell you that it constantly smells of urine."

Paris is off the list.

He couldn't help but crack a smirk. There was something about her opinionated forthrightness that made a conversation with her a little different from one with most women.

"Again," he said. "You can reach one of us at that number. If we aren't available, there will still be a detective to take your call, day or night. And if you think of something else, don't hesitate to let one of us know."

Rose tugged on the collar of her nightgown, pulling it tight at the top. "Have you been doing this very long, Detective Palmer?"

"I've put a lot of guilty people in jail if that's what you're asking."

"And how many in the ground?" Rose asked.

Frank paused. "Less than that," he said. "I prefer to let justice take care of itself if at all possible."

She accompanied him to the door. "I hope you find whoever did this, detective."

"I will." He circled to address her once again from the hallway. "You can be sure of that." He tipped his hat to the lovely lady and listened for the door to close behind him.

He then heard the sound of the lock being turned.

On his way to the elevator, Palmer mulled over their discussion. He didn't have any reason to doubt her story. It seemed solid, and it would take more acting chops than she had to have pulled off that kind of performance. Besides, she didn't appear to understand the gravity of the situation—just throwing Arturo Casadonte's name out there like that. But if Maxwell's death were over debt, she wouldn't have anything to worry about, especially since she wasn't involved in those affairs.

He took a ride back to the ground floor with the elevator man, who was still of the elated disposition Palmer had last seen him in. Exiting the building, the smell of morning was in the air. People getting out of church started to fill the sidewalks and streets, as well as those who had simply had a late Saturday night.

With the city coming to life, Palmer had no impulse to regard the two men watching him from the car parked across the street.

"That's a cop." The passenger leaned over the driver, looking through the window.

"How can you tell?" The driver watched Palmer open the door and get into his own car.

"Just look at him, Joey. It ain't that hard to figure out."

"The hell's he doing here? You think she knows something? And if she does—think she's squealing?"

"We need to let this place cool down—get out of here—come back after dark."

After watching Palmer's black Buick pull away, the two men agitated by his presence left in the opposite direction.

FIVE

NOW WAS NOT THE TIME to be pushing Benny Cassano's buttons. Bitter Benny achieved the custom-tailored nickname due to the perpetual resting scowl he wore—perhaps the only thing he had ever earned honestly. He was nearly as short as he was wide and had no neck to speak of—just a square shaped head sitting atop a broad torso. The way he wore his hat nearly over his eyes gave the impression that he didn't have any eyebrows, which did no favors in adding to his image.

But he was a snappy dresser. He had three different business suits he preferred to rotate, and each of those had its own mannequin that modeled them better than Benny.

Joey Donati was physically the opposite of Benny. He was thin and elongated, with a slender nose that projected well beyond the rest of his gaunt facial structure.

Being the only man whose features were more rodent-like than his, Gyp Lucetti had always enjoyed a little fun at Joey's expense. He once withdrew a stack of money from a brown envelope, separating it into two piles on the table. In an attempt to further antagonize Joey, Lucetti obnoxiously announced to everyone present that if Joey could guess how much money was on the table, he could have it.

To everyone's surprise, Joey did exactly that, earning himself twelve hundred thirty dollars in the process, and Joey Two Stacks was born that day.

Dusk stretched across the city, and by the time the two men left Season Heights, they would be able to do so under the cover of night.

"You okay?" Joey asked. "You look a little tense."

"That cop being here sure raised his blood pressure when we told him," Benny said as they approached the building.

Joey knew where to draw the line when it came to asking the boss questions, but he was well aware of how quickly the situation had escalated. "Did you see his face?"

Benny agreed. "Now I bet he really wonders what she knows."

After they had watched Palmer leaving the apartment complex, the two strong arms returned to report their findings, and the police presence was something their employer found more than disconcerting.

In an ideal situation, they would get into the house and rummage through Maxwell's study, but that wasn't going to be an option—the police had the entire property locked down and had a twenty-four-hour watch posted on the premises. This left having an impolite conversation with Maxwell's old flame as a second best option. Maybe she knew the details their employer wanted to remain a secret—maybe she didn't—but nevertheless, it had fallen on Benny and Joey to find out what that was.

Joey rubbed his chin. "Do you even know what we're supposed to be looking for?"

When Benny shrugged, the rising of his broad shoulders made it appear as if his head were sinking into his body, threatening to disappear within his coat.

"Something to do with records he kept," Benny said. "I don't know. But trust me, once we start putting on the heat, she'll tell us everything she knows, even if we don't know the questions to the answers we're looking for. Any time it gets them out of trouble, women will always sing. They don't call them birds for nothing."

Joey nodded to the doorman when they crossed the threshold of the apartment building. "I wish we could just get some of the boys together and blaze our way into Maxwell's place. Might be a hell of a lot easier than getting the truth out of a dame."

"Have you lost all your marbles or is there just a hole in the bag?" Benny smacked Joey's arm with the back of his hand. "Discretion is the whole point of this operation. And waging war on the cops ain't no one's idea of being discreet on any day of the week."

"I wasn't serious." Joey feigned dejection. "I just said I wish."

The men paused their conversation when the elevator operator appeared and closed the door behind them.

"How are you gentlemen this evening?" George King asked.

Neither man answered.

"Me?" The elderly man grinned and continued to talk to the air. "It's just the best day of my life."

Benny kept his gaze forward, not even bothering to look at the attendant. "Look, we ain't in the mood for conversation. So, if you want it to stay that way, just shut your yap and let us get to where we're going."

"Eleventh floor," Joey said.

Once they had arrived at their destination, the two men marched the hallway until they reached the apartment they were looking for.

"You want to do the honors?" Benny asked.

* * * * *

Sometime in the early afternoon, Roselyn Farrell had found the will to get dressed. She didn't have any plans on going out that evening, but she expected a warm bath and making herself presentable would make some progress toward helping her to feel better.

Rose had been able to keep the dress worn on the set—a red garment that fell just below the knees and buttoned down the center in the front. She didn't remember what happened to the hat. Rose wasn't able to find it the day the production wrapped.

After pouring her fourth drink of the day, she wondered if some music would distract her for awhile, but thought better of it when she realized there was likely going to be a tribute to her estranged lover playing on the radio throughout the day.

Rose wasn't expecting any visitors, but when the knock came, Rose managed a smile for the first time that day. Maybe that charming and brawny detective wanted that drink after all.

The life was struck from the smile on Rose's face when she opened the door to discover no handsome man to be found among the pair.

"Good evening, miss." Joey removed his hat, "If you don't mind, we'd like to come in. We're going to need to ask you some questions."

Roselyn Farrell regarded Benny and Joey with slight disappointment. "I've already spoken with Detective Palmer this morning. Was there something else that came to light?"

Benny pushed Roselyn back inside with one arm as he barged into the apartment, taking her off balance.

Joey followed and closed the door behind them, twisting the lock.

Benny shoved Roselyn into the chair, which padded her fall, but she rose slightly in defiance. "What do you think you're doing? I assure you, Detective Palmer will hear of this."

"Shut up," Benny barked. "We ain't detectives."

The two men created a semicircle before her. Joey began the interrogation. "This cop—Palmer—what did you tell him?"

"I told him the contents of my Eiffel Tower snow globe may as well be yellow."

"Oh, you're a funny one," Benny oozed with sarcasm. "Too bad your picture wasn't with William Powell." He pointed to the poster on the wall. "You might have made a name for yourself in comedy that way."

"Look," Joey admitted, "We don't want to have to rough you up, so don't make it come to that. Just answer the questions, tell us what we want to know, and we'll be out of your pretty hair."

"And your beautiful face will stay that way," Benny added.

Rose's heart rate increased. These men were serious. Although they had threatened violence, they hadn't acted upon it yet. But that may have been only a matter of time.

There was no way to get to the phone, and they stood between her and the door. She wasn't going anywhere.

"So," Joey said. "Let's just all play nice here. We're just like your pals coming over for a visit. You can tell us what's going on in your life—we'd especially like to hear the latest juicy gossip."

Benny gave Joey a sore look. Sometimes he wondered if Joey had the guts to do what needed to be done when it came down to it. He talked big about having shootouts with the cops, but he wondered if that was mere puffery.

"That's right," Benny said through his teeth. "We're going to play it nice. Now, I'm going to ask you again, sweetheart—what did that cop want?"

Maybe she could stall them. But what would she be stalling them for? If she told them everything, then the sooner they would be gone. Maybe. But what would happen when they had all the answers—when the questioning was finished—where would that leave her?

"I think he suspected me in Morgan's death."

Benny burst into laughter. "He did, did he? Now that's a funny thing to imagine—a cute little broad like you blasting gats."

Joey grinned. "You said it yourself—she might have made a career in comedy."

"Try again." Benny's face became one of seriousness. "Because I'm only going to ask you with my words one more time."

"Gambling." Rose turned her blue eyes upward. "Something to do with gambling."

"Maxwell owe someone a bunch of money?" Joey asked.

"Someone," Rose said. "He thought it could have had something to do with the types of clubs Morgan frequented."

"Like seedy type places?" Benny asked.

"Exactly those types of places."

"Did he say any names? Have any evidence? Suspects?" Joey pressed.

"No, he didn't know any of the clubs by name. We went to so many, I could have just told him every club in town that had a card table."

Benny nodded slowly, pushing his hat over his eyebrows. He turned to Joey. "You know what? I could use a drink. Why don't you go make us one? It's starting to look like we're getting somewhere, and I wouldn't mind a little relaxation."

Joey went to the bar and perused the contents, finding a common theme. "Jeez, lady, you sure do like brandy."

He retrieved two glasses, filling them with the dark liquor. "I'm going to make myself one, too if you don't mind." It wasn't a request.

Now was her chance. Roselyn made a break for the door. Standing and moving with all her weight in one fluid motion, she shoved Benny as hard as she could.

She had a grip on the handle before two strong hands squeezed her shoulders, jerking her back roughly. She stumbled and lost one of her heels, and looked up just in time to receive the back of Benny's hand across her deep red mouth.

The sting forced a cry from her lips, and Rose went down on the rug. Holding her face, tears began to form.

"That was foolish." Benny pulled the collar of his coat down as he paced.

Joey left the two glasses unattended and reached into his jacket for his piece.

As he approached, Benny grabbed Rose underneath the arms and lifted her from the floor, throwing her back into the chair. Joey had to catch the back of it to keep her from tipping over from the force.

"Kill the lights and close those curtains," Benny said coldly. "We don't want someone across the way seeing this."

Feeling a tinge of remorse, Joey flipped the light switch as he approached the window, filling the room with the moonlight of dusk. He didn't know what was going to happen to her next. As he went to take the drapes in hand, Joey looked across to the building beyond the darkness, but his view was blocked by something coming at him too fast to react.

Benny whirled around in surprise as the window exploded and a figure dressed entirely in black landed hard atop Joey, sending his .45 skidding across the hardwood floor.

The weight of the man knocked the wind from Joey's lungs, and he wasn't sure if he had glass in his eyes or if he was cut and it was his own blood that was blinding him.

The moment Benny had his pistol from its holster, a gloved hand closed over it. The gun roared, and the flash from the barrel briefly reflected on the man's face like that of a bonfire ghost story.

Twisting violently, the man in black caused the audible sound of broken fingers, forcing Benny to drop the gun.

The figure kicked the pistol away from Benny's reach as Joey rolled over and wiped the blood from his face.

Eyes wide and brows raised high, Rose couldn't move. The chair held her safely in place like an amusement park ride. There was no participation—no reaction—all she could do was experience.

Rushing the man, Joey crashed awkwardly on the wooden floor, lying in more glass, hurled over the attacker's shoulder and landing on the coffee table.

Benny nursed his broken hand close to his body, but Joey's predicament incited him to act. He swung with his good hand, but the intended target blocked with his forearm, returning fire with a hook to the ribs that almost took Benny down.

The pistol Benny had dropped was closer, and Joey scrambled for it, but he only came close to the object of his desire before it was kicked away again. A hand grabbed his collar and bade him to rise.

The uppercut caught Joey flush on the chin, sending him sprawling backward, where he knocked over the two stools at the bar.

Benny grabbed him from behind, but the man in black threw his head back, spreading Benny's nose across his face. He turned and delivered a right cross that shattered teeth and turned out Benny's lights.

The intruder then directed his attention toward the paralyzed blonde held in the chair's invisible grip.

Rose looked upon the man breathlessly, her mouth agape. The scant lighting hid the strangely shaped face she had only seen from the earlier muzzle flash. She attempted to speak, but the words wouldn't come out.

As the man crept closer, his shadow became a giant cast over Rose as she withdrew, sliding into the back of the chair.

He tipped his hat to her politely.

"Miss."

SIX

Monday, April 12, 1937.

THE ONLY FAILURE he had ever known to burn was the one wrenching the inside of his ailing heart. Nicodemus Crocetti had often questioned whether it would give out on him before everything had been seen to fruition.

There were many things in life orchestrated to bring worry: the passing of his brother-in-law, the state of the economy, the other families in the city and the rising taxes.

But nothing concerned him more than the uncertain future that lay in wait for him within the next room.

He appreciated the reverence that came with being Nico Crocetti. When he spoke, people listened. When he asked questions, they answered. And when he was fueled by ire, they shut up.

What he didn't treasure about being Nico Crocetti were the small moments like now—the times when people were summoned for an audience and then sat in his office and then told him only what he wanted to hear—or worse, a half-truth of convenience—instead of the reality of a situation.

Watching from the tenth floor of his building, the business of life took place below, unaware that their daily routines were being watched from on high by a power that shaped the city and everything around them.

He finally turned from the window, facing the two men again. "You don't agree."

There was no mistaking that the Depression hadn't taken any food from Calvin Arnold's table. He shifted in his chair and twisted the edge of his mustache, which was a habit he often exhibited coinciding with discomfort.

Calvin pondered the other man, and then assessed Crocetti, tugging on the knot of his necktie with one finger. "Sir?"

"Contradictions," Crocetti said flatly. "One of you comes every Tuesday and tells me one thing, and the other shows up on Thursday and tells me something different. And now it's Monday, and the three of us are going to have an answer—or at least I am—before you leave this office. Because I'm not playing that game again this week."

Kent Roth looked like he could have been a veteran of the Civil War and though his services came with the highest recommendation, it was only now that Crocetti was beginning to doubt his heralded abilities.

"Mr. Crocetti," Roth said. "This is a—delicate issue. I don't know about Mr. Arnold— "

"Doctor," Arnold corrected.

"Yes, of course." Roth cleared his throat. "But I have seen significant signs of improvement from the previous weeks up until last week."

Arnold spoke as if Roth were not in the room. "I have not."

"And this right here is what I mean. A difference of opinion. I've done everything you've told me to do, except put on face paint and shake a feather totem dancing around in moccasins with a grass skirt that doesn't cover my ass. Should I be doing that next?"

"Now, Mr. Crocetti, I don't think that will be— "

"Shut up, Kent." Nico pointed a finger. "That was rhetorical. I'm not talking magic juju here, I want science. Medicine—answers—God damn results. Stop butting heads. You're going to be working together from now on. Do either of you snake oil salesmen get what I'm saying?"

"As Dr. Roth advised, this is an issue of a most delicate nature," Calvin Arnold said. "Because I'll be honest, Mr. Crocetti..."

Arnold's pause was the inconvenient opportunity for Crocetti to interject. He threw his hands into the air as he sat on the edge of his desk.

"Oh, so now you're going to be honest, are you, doctor? That's you now—Honest Arnold."

Roth shook his head and signaled for Arnold to wait. "Mr. Crocetti, I understand your frustration. But until we've been able to run more tests, I don't know if we'll be able to have any conclusive diagnoses for you. I think Dr. Arnold will agree that this is unlike anything we've encountered in the past."

Calvin Arnold nodded. "That I do."

Roth expressed concern. "However, Mr. Crocetti, I think it would be more comfortable to move things back to the house like before."

"No, we won't be doing that. The hotel is working just fine," Crocetti said, circling his desk. "So here's what we're going to do now... You're not competing. You two are partners now, as far as I'm concerned. So this teamwork begins immediately, and you either succeed or fail together."

Roth agreed as Arnold remained in thought, twisting his mustache. "I do have two appointments I need to tend to this morning before we begin."

"They're canceled," Crocetti said. "You can call on them tomorrow. I know for a fact I pay you more in a month than those two patients combined will pay you all year. Unless you're telling me now that some little oath you suddenly feel the need to uphold is more important than the fat wads I keep stuffing in your seemingly bottomless pockets on a weekly basis."

Arnold cleared his throat. "About that, sir. I have not heard from your man in two weeks. Please excuse my forthrightness— "

"There he is again with the honesty." Crocetti's patience was beginning to draw thin. "Don't worry, Calvin, you'll get your money. I'll send Mickey Clean over this afternoon, and he'll settle you up."

"Thank you, Mr. Crocetti."

A knock on the door announced the arrival of Crocetti's valet. He entered the office, his entire upper body completely obscured by the massive bouquet of a multi-colored flower arrangement he carried. "A delivery for you, sir."

Crocetti took the vase. "Thank you, Paulson. Did you cut the ends off?"

"I did, sir."

He imagined Paulson had a better recollection of how long he had worked for him. Crocetti knew that of all his men, Paulson had been around the longest. There were others before that, but they didn't have the same staying power—and their jobs were often considered more dangerous. Paulson wasn't involved in many affairs that would land him behind bars or in the earth. Usually.

"They live longer if you do that," Crocetti said to Arnold and Roth. "You snip the tips off the bottom, and they keep soaking up water for awhile."

Whether or not they were aware of this, neither doctor had an opinion on the matter.

"Hold any calls or visitors until I say otherwise, Paulson."

"Of course, sir."

When the valet was gone, Crocetti continued to hold the bouquet, speaking to the doctors with his head cranked around the side of the arrangement.

"You both have all your notes and files with you?"

They answered in the affirmative.

"Good. Compare those and see what you can figure out while I'm gone. I'll come back when I'm ready for you."

* * * * *

Leaving his office, Crocetti closed the door behind him and maneuvered the familiar hallway. These flowers would be perfect. They were more colorful than last time and had a discernible fragrance about them. The florist charged an arm and a leg, and Nico was pretty sure the price had steadily risen, but maybe that wasn't so much him being taken for a ride as it was excise taxes.

He opened the bedroom door as quietly as possible.

She was already awake and sitting upright in the bed, pillows behind her back. Even though her attire consisted of a nightgown most days now, Myrna was just as lovely as the day he had first seen her.

"Good morning, my dear," Nico said as he entered, holding the flowers with outstretched arms to show them off.

"Oh, those are beautiful," Myrna said, her voice unsteady. "Almost as pretty as yesterday."

He sat the vase on the nightstand. "And you, my dear, are even more beautiful than yesterday." Nico approached, delivering a soft kiss on her forehead as she stretched upward expectantly.

"The doctors are here," he noted.

"It's Thursday already? I hadn't realized."

Nico could tell that although she slept the entire night, she was still tired.

He sat down on the bed, taking her delicate hand in both of his. "You needn't concern yourself with such trivial things, darling. You just need to rest and recover your strength."

Myrna smiled. "What did I ever do to deserve a perfect life such as this?"

Crocetti didn't want the frown on his face to give away his true feelings, so he removed it as quickly as possible. His beautiful wife was forced to stay in bed most days, yet she never allowed the fatigue and discomfort to get the best of her spirit. She was a strong one, and so he had to remain stalwart as well.

"How is it this morning?" Nico asked.

"My muscles feel fine, so far. There's no pain in the joints, either, so I thought I'd get up and walk around in a little while." Myrna's feet kicked at the blankets covering her lower half. "I'm hot."

"Here, let me," Nico said. He drew the thick blankets to the end of the bed. "I could walk with you. Maybe we could even take a stroll through the garden."

She laughed, looking around the room. "I would wager that you've brought most of the garden to me."

Although the vases that littered the room didn't hold contents from the garden, Nico had ensured there was an ever-present cornucopia of her favorites on permanent display.

"It does seem that way, sometimes." Nico caressed her thigh fondly through the silken material.

"No," Myrna said, "It's okay. I'll have Adelaide walk with me. I think the halls will be enough for me today."

"You shouldn't depend on her too much," Nico warned. "The more you can do for yourself, the more you'll start to feel better."

Her stern look locked his gaze with hers. "I don't depend on her, Nico—she just helps."

Nico knew he wasn't going to win that argument, so he offered no protest.

"It's just as it's always been," she said. "Except that she does a little more now. She's still the best maidservant I've ever had, and I'd love to put two more just like her to work for me. There are so many things I can think of to be done at home—I would make sure they fully earned their five dollars each week."

Nico rose to open the curtains. The window was on the west wall so the light would look nice, but not beam in directly on her. "It's a shame the factory isn't running as efficiently."

"It's the unions," she said.

Crocetti sighed, "I know. I'm working on that."

"I'm pretty sure over there they practice workers' confiscation."

"What?" Nico knew that confusion came with her condition sometimes, but now he found himself that way. "I think you mean workers' compensation."

"No, I said what I meant. We can barely afford to keep the factory open, and they believe they have the right to be lazy and still remain employed. Now they've adopted the attitude that if they get paid so much per day, then they're going to only do what they view to be that amount's worth of work per day—workers' confiscation."

Nico not only admired Myrna's beauty to no measure but her intelligence, as well. She was truly the smartest woman he had ever known.

"I know you miss being there," he said.

"I do." She looked upward to him. "Jimmy is a fine supervisor, but I love seeing how much more productive they are when I'm there."

"Well," he said, grinning, "I'm sure once the doctors get this thing figured out, you'll be back there cracking the whip two days a week in no time."

"That would be lovely," Myrna said, frowning.

Nico noted the expression as he returned to her bedside. "What's wrong?"

"What are we going to do? The factory. It's going to go under any day now, and you're spending all this money on doctors." She swept her arm across the bedroom. "And flowers."

"You let me worry about that," Nico said. "As soon as the executor gets Sal's will all sorted out, there won't be anything for you to fret over. And I'll get rid of those two and make sure you have the best doctors in the country."

The funeral had been scheduled for later that afternoon. He knew Myrna wouldn't be able to attend, so Nico hadn't bothered telling her about it. He had never wished his brother-in-law ill, but Salvadore Barone's passing couldn't have come at a better time, as far as financial conditions were concerned.

"If it gets too bad in the meantime, maybe we could sell to Casadonte..."

Nico scowled. "I wouldn't sell Arturo Casadonte an ashtray for a motorcycle. His lawyer, Florian—that big-spending smiling jackass—tried to make a lowball offer two weeks ago. I have some other things in the works, too—we're making new friends these days—so we're just going to tough it out with the factory and ride this thing through. Besides, I know you'll want to get all dolled up and go evaluate the production once you get to feeling better."

"Well," her ruby lips curled into a smile, "If the affairs of the will seem to be taking too long, we know Florian is a big gambler—maybe you can have him lay some money on the table and get Joey Donati to guess how much is there."

The sound of her laughter ringing through the room on one of her good days was positively delightful.

SEVEN

THE HOUSE WAS ALWAYS quiet this time of morning. The businessman—he wore his gray suit today—would kiss his wife goodbye around seven-thirty and about an hour later, the wife would leave to go to an unknown elsewhere. This left the old white domicile alone on the rising hill, its windows gazing upon the black Buick parked on the outer side of the quiet two-lane residential street below.

Palmer blew white smoke through the half-cracked window as he leaned back in the seat and looked at his watch. He still had ten minutes.

The house was old but still looked to be in good condition from the outside. Constructed in the late 1800s, the residence had a full front porch that wrapped around three-quarters of the house. Palmer looked upon it fondly as he enjoyed the silence of the street—it had always been a good place for him to park and think—never changing from the first time he had done it.

He grabbed one of the ledger books from the passenger's side and flipped it open. Callaghan had thoroughly gone through both books yesterday morning, making his own notes and observations on every page. He probably had the best penmanship Palmer had ever seen. It was clearly differential to Maxwell's scrawl and didn't look like the writing of someone who was related to a doctor—block letters in black, scribed with steady hands.

The book was filled with annotations and questions. The most apparent recurrence was an attempt to determine which of the reputed bosses was referred to as "Mr. C." Maxwell had also spent a good portion of money on flowers, but the florist was one of the listings that there was no effort to hide. Every two weeks, Tammary's Floral was listed without fail.

Tammary's Floral was owned by two sisters—Tamara and Mary—who had gone into business together at the beginning of the twenties. Never having decided on a proper name for their shop, the sisters had decided to combine their names, since the result sounded a little like someone's last name. It was one of the longest-standing and most notable shops in the lower east side, and even Palmer himself had experience in dealing with the sisters in the past.

Not only did Mary and Tamara have the greenest thumbs in the city, but the ladies were polite and pleasant company to be around, putting their renowned customer service above all else—probably even more important than being the muses of things that grow. Even the gangsters loved them—that was probably even the majority of their business and another part of the reason the independent businesswomen had become so successful during the last fifteen years. It was likely the only place in town that two rival mob members could inhabit at the same time and remain cordial. It was no secret that every mobster had a girlfriend or three they liked to keep happy.

As happy as those kinds of girls can be.

There was even talk that Mary and Tamara were discussing the possibility of publishing a magazine sometime later that year.

Palmer tossed his cigarette and opened the silver case, considering smoking another as he perused the ledger books. Only three left. He closed the cigarette case and put it back in his coat pocket, hoping he would remember to get more later.

As he reached the end of the ledger book from thirty-five, he saw for himself—as well as Callaghan's notes—that the details ended abruptly in November.

Maybe his Christmas list was even more secretive than his mob dealings.

Palmer smirked at the thought and wondered the same thing Callaghan withheld because it was obvious—why was the ledger book from thirty-six missing? It could have just been an oversight, or maybe it just wasn't in his study. Perhaps it was even ashes in the bottom of Maxwell's fireplace.

Roselyn Farrell seemed on the up and up, though. Her good looks—which she had in spades—was enough to probably keep most men from looking any deeper, but Palmer wasn't one to just be mesmerized by a pretty face. They were everywhere—she wasn't the only one—and certainly wouldn't be the last he saw. He also had the feeling it wouldn't be the last of her that he saw, either.

He checked his watch again and started the car. Taking one more look at the white house, he gave the strong old friend the nod and pressed the accelerator.

From the residential street, he was able to take some of the back roads to the station, avoiding most of the morning commuters in the process.

He could already see Callaghan's face. He would ask about the ledger books as though Palmer had memorized his detailed notes. A feeling of dread rose within him—he hadn't even opened the other ledger yet. He barely remembered what it was like, though—waking up every morning and leaping into the shoes you would wear to walk the fine lines of justice.

They're practically dancing shoes at first.

Callaghan would get over it in time.

Finding a parking spot was relatively easy this morning. Most of the other detectives either hadn't made it in or had already hit the streets, depending on how new they were.

On his way up the steps, he responded to the uniforms that acknowledged him and was then bum-rushed by Callaghan before he could even get fully in the door.

"Don't you ever answer your phone?" Callaghan looked like a lost puppy. He was almost bouncing with fervor, wringing his hands.

"I looked at them, Callaghan. But I still need some time to—"

"She's here, Palmer. Last night. All kinds of heck in all sorts of places. You're not going to believe this." Callaghan waved for Palmer to follow, walking briskly down the hall and talking over his shoulder.

Frank sped up to keep from being left behind. "Who? What the hell's going on?"

"Roselyn Farrell. She says two men came to her apartment last night and smacked her around, asking questions..."

"They what?" Palmer clenched his fist, feeling his body temperature rise from the neck up. "God damn it—is she all right?"

"She's a little bruised, but she's fine. Know why? Because a man in black with a reflective mask busted up the party and gave these two guys the what for."

"She saw him?" Palmer's eyes widened.

They rounded the hall and arrived at one of the interrogation rooms.

"Yeah," Callaghan said. "She says he smashed right through her window."

"That's on the eleventh floor."

"I know. He must have used the fire escape. She says she stayed in a hotel last night, but won't say anything else. I told her I was your partner, but she wants to talk to you specifically. I was about to come get you again."

Callaghan opened the door, revealing the blonde in the room. She was dressed in that red dress from the movie poster. When she saw Palmer, Roselyn Farrell was ejected from the chair, wrapping her arms around him.

Frank held his arms aloft at first but finally gave her a gentle pat on the back. Taking her by the shoulders, he brought her so that they could look eye to eye. "Are you okay?"

"I don't know who they were—what they wanted. They were asking about Morgan. And then that man from the stories— "

"Just—just calm down, Miss Farrell. Everything's going to be all right now. My partner here will get you some coffee." Palmer glanced at Callaghan, who nodded and made his way to the exit.

Rose raised a finger. "Do you have tea?"

Charlie took a softer tone than normal. "Sure, I'll see what I can find."

When the door closed, Palmer pulled up a chair beside Roselyn, so that they were seated facing each other with the chairs in a v-formation.

"It was awful," she said. "I've never been so scared in my life. I wanted to come to the station, but I knew you wouldn't be here. So I stayed at the hotel until morning. I didn't sleep at all."

The puffiness of her face was not only from crying or lack of sleep. One cheek was bruised, just underneath her eye, and that side of her lip was swollen as well.

"You said you don't know who they were?" Palmer asked.

Rose shook her head. "No, I've never seen them before."

"Not at one of the clubs? Not at a gathering? Nowhere?"

"I don't know who they were. I told you, I've never seen them until last night."

Palmer sat back in the chair. "Did they identify one another in any way? Maybe one of them slipped a name?"

"I don't remember. I don't think so."

Being able to put a name to one of the two men would have gone a long way toward not only figuring out who they were but possibly discovering who was behind Maxwell's murder. But these two were either talented or lucky—they could have even been professionals. But from the sounds of things, they would now have markings that would make them easier to identify.

The door opened, and Callaghan came back into the room empty handed. Rose and Frank turned to him, filled with expectations.

"Where's the tea?" Palmer threw a hand out.

"I've got one of the uniforms on it. I thought you might need me here."

"Yeah," Palmer said. "Neither of the goons dropped any names—she doesn't know who they are. That's as far as I got."

Palmer stood up and began pacing the room while Callaghan took the seat he had previously occupied.

"Do you think anyone else saw these guys?" Callaghan asked Palmer.

"I don't know," Palmer considered. "Wait, there was that elevator man…"

"George King," Roselyn said.

Palmer glanced to Callaghan. "We'll talk to him when we go have a look at the apartment."

"What did they ask specifically?" Charlie inquired. "They had to be there for something."

Rose rubbed her tired eyes, dry and reddened from the absence of sleep. "Something about documents Morgan had."

"The ledger books?" Callaghan glanced up to Palmer.

Frank ceased his pacing, arms behind his back. "Probably." He then asked Rose, "Did Maxwell ever leave any of these with you, by chance?"

Rose shook her head. "That's what they were trying to find out, I think. I know he had them in his study, but he never brought them over. Why do you ask?"

Before he could be stopped by the cold look Palmer shot at him, Charlie said, "There's one missing." This was at the same moment that Frank responded, "Just wondering."

The awkward moment was broken by the arrival of a uniformed officer. He carried a steaming coffee mug in his hand. Clearing his throat, he apologized. "We didn't have any tea cups, ma'am."

Roselyn took the mug graciously, sipping at the edge.

Callaghan offered thanks to the officer and ushered him back out the door. As he closed it, the uniform's gaze fell on Roselyn as if she were familiar to him, but he couldn't place where he'd seen her before.

Roselyn managed a smile as he closed the door behind him.

When the uniform got outside, they heard his voice echo through the halls as he announced to everyone, "Hey, I think I just saw Jocelyn Farrell!"

Frank removed his hat and smoothed his dark hair as Callaghan resumed the interview.

"So, these guys—guys you've never seen before—came in and roughed you up, asking questions. What happened after that?"

She turned her eyes to the floor, replaying the incident in her mind. "I don't know what it—he—was. He came through the window from nowhere and landed on the tall one. It was like he was—I don't know—born from shadow. I know that sounds crazy."

Palmer withdrew from the interview and allowed Callaghan to take over fully, watching carefully as Rose recounted the story of how Mortuary entered her apartment and took it to the two aggressors. The description was exactly as Palmer remembered it. It had to be him.

"One of the men tried to shoot him," she said. "But he was able to stop it. I think it hit the sofa and something near the bar—I heard glass shatter."

"Were you able to see his face?" Callaghan asked.

"No," she said. "It was covered by something. It was dark, but the light from the window reflected off it. Like it was rubber or metal or something." Rose was lost in the distance for a moment. "He didn't even lose his hat..."

Palmer rejoined the conversation. "What?"

"Coming through the window—the fight—and leaving. The entire time, his hat stayed on his head."

Callaghan looked at Palmer. "Rubber seal. Like what fall guys use to keep their hats on in the pictures—especially in the old west movies."

"Did he say anything?" Palmer asked.

"He just—tipped the brim of his hat—I think he addressed me in a polite manner and then—he leaned backward and just fell back through the window."

Frank nodded to Callaghan. "We're going to go have a look around your apartment. In the meantime, we'll have them take care of the hotel you stayed at last night—at least for the next few days. Keep you out of sight and out of harm's way while we figure this thing out."

EIGHT

WHEN HE TESTED THE HANDLE, Palmer learned that he wouldn't need the key Roselyn had provided. No doubt she was in a hurry to leave in the aftermath of the incident.

Callaghan gave Palmer a look of warning and drew his pistol, prompting the larger man to nod and follow suit, pulling Maurice from the holster.

With weapons at the ready, Palmer pushed the door open, and Callaghan entered first. Charlie leveled his pistol and slowly swept the front room, with Palmer following closely behind.

Frank closed the door and turned the lock, just in case any unwanted visitors returned while they were skulking about.

The apartment was a mess. Broken glass covered the floor near the large window, one of the soft chairs was overturned on its side, and the two stools at the bar matched the disarray.

Callaghan gestured for Palmer to proceed. Frank had been to the apartment before and would be more familiar with the layout and the likelihood of locales where any remnants of intrusion could successfully hide.

The other side of the bar was clear, save for a few broken bottles and the men soon determined that the bedroom and bathroom held no signs of life, either.

"You said he was retiring?" Callaghan asked as he turned off the light in the bathroom.

"Who?" Frank put his weapon away.

Callaghan took the cue, doing the same. "The elevator man, George King."

"Yeah. Said it was his last night." Palmer maneuvered back toward the front of the apartment. "The main attraction happened in the living room."

Callaghan waved his hand across the area of the floor like a stage illusionist perpetrating the art of distraction.

"I already see one—two—bullet casings."

The location of one of the casings was in plain sight, resting in the open near the overturned chair. The other lay beside one of the front legs of the sofa.

"She said one of the guys discharged his weapon while they were fighting," Palmer recalled.

Frowning, Frank saw that the snow globe atop the mantle had been destroyed in the scuffle. The glass and water were equally spread on the mantle as they were on the floor. The miniature tower that was once inside couldn't be located from his current field of vision.

"They had to be strong arms," Callaghan said.

Palmer agreed, finally seeing that the little Eiffel Tower had been knocked at least eight feet away from the mantle and was lying near the bar.

Callaghan pulled the cushions from the sofa, noting a bullet hole in the back of the fine piece of furnishing as they continued to scour the apartment. "You said she mentioned Arturo Casadonte the first time you talked with her. That could have been who sent these guys."

"She did," Palmer said. "But I don't know what would make anyone think she was responsible for any outstanding debt Maxwell had brought to his own table."

A gust of morning breeze caused a few of the remaining fragments to fall from the window pane, drawing their attention.

"And this..." Callaghan gestured toward the window. "What do you think of the arrival of this so-called man in black?"

"He had great timing. Can also handle himself pretty well."

Charlie tossed the cushions back onto the sofa. "You know what I mean. And you know who they're going to say it was if this manages to find a way into the official report."

Palmer ignored Callaghan's skepticism. "This guy climbed all the way up here—that's at least a hundred feet. Then he comes through the window, gives two other men a lesson in pugilism and jumps back out the window. He probably used the fire escape somehow to get down. Otherwise, there would be an ink blot down there. Still... Sounds like him to me."

Snatching up the casing near the chair, Callaghan turned to his partner. "I heard you saw him at Rohde Falls."

Palmer nodded. "Yeah. A few months ago—not too long before your wedding."

Waiting for Palmer to continue, it was a moment before he realized that he was going to have to follow up if he wanted the discussion to proceed.

"I've read the stories in *The Amendment*, and I'll tell you, they range from something that sounds pretty reasonable to the border of where ridiculous meets crazy. And the quality of the witnesses—who all declined to give their names—that doesn't help, either."

"Some outdoorsman found a body in the woods just southwest of the city, near Rohde Falls—female and unidentifiable—probably a gal who wasn't lucky enough to have anyone who was looking for her. A few weeks later, a girl who did have that went missing. There was no ransom letter, no demands, but without a body, her family was pretty determined that she had been kidnapped. There wasn't any reason for her to just run off, and she didn't have any previous men in her life with any kind of history of the morally lacking variety."

"That sounds familiar," Callaghan said. "It seems like I saw her face in the paper. Her family put up a reward, right?"

"Yeah, they did," Palmer recalled the scene that had been burned into his memory. "You know how it goes. He showed up last year. At first, it was just the word of a few pretty unreliable witnesses—just like you said—a vagrant who claimed he just swooped out of the night and put lead into two men wanted for murder. After a couple more sightings, the newspapers decided they were linked, so they put a name to a face no one had seen."

"Seems like they ran a story about it every couple weeks after that."

In the months since earning a moniker that would cause even the most robust of wills to waver with a sense of unease, it was revealed that Mortuary created victims from those who victimized.

"According to the story, he started amassing a nice little body count," Palmer said. "A collection of expired killers and rapists who soured the world a little more just by being in it—especially the ones who didn't just do those types of things to adults."

"And none of these men he came after lived to talk about it?"

"I'm not crying for them," Palmer admitted. "Anyway, this girl had gone missing. I forget her name—some brunette in her twenties. She wasn't anyone important in the grand scheme, really—like a congressman's daughter— "

Callaghan collected the other casing and wrapped them both in a handkerchief, twisting the top and shoving it in his pocket. "Or a former Hollywood starlet?"

"Just like that." Palmer turned the cushioned chair upright. "But it was the perpetrator that was so damn weird. He was a respected scientist in his field and part of an elite group of thinkers. He didn't have any criminal history and everyone we interviewed later had nothing but the highest regard for the guy. It was like he was perfectly normal one day—and then just had some kind of breakdown."

"My father used to always say that stress is never the blessed bride of eccentricity."

"Well, this guy had clearly gone over the edge. I ended up tracking him to an old farmhouse his family had just outside the city. I waited until dark, but the door was locked, so I let myself in anyway. As soon as I walked in the door, it smelled like shit."

It was the only clue Palmer needed to know that sinister intentions had been in play for some time.

"Like a body?" The glass from the window crunched beneath his shoes as Callaghan inspected the fire escape.

"Like a house full of bodies. I drew my sidearm and tried my best to sneak up the stairs, but the first one creaked like a whistle, and I figured that was the end of my element of surprise."

Upstairs, the lamentations of a woman struggling echoed throughout the house, her moans and grunts indicating that she was resisting some sort of restraint.

"Then I heard what sounded like a man weeping." Palmer completed his stairway ascent into a deeper darkness and entered the room with caution, pistol at the ready. "When I stepped into the room, there he was, holding a forty-five on a man pleading for his life, kneeling on the floor."

"The scientist?" Callaghan casually deduced from the obvious.

"Yeah, the kidnapper. Mortuary is wearing this long black coat and a hat. His face and head were covered in what looks to me like some sort of gas mask—completely obscured. When he spoke, his voice sounded kind of like— like it was coming through a radio with bad reception, marred by static."

"He actually broke silence to you? What did he say?"

"He looked right at me. Then he said, 'In vita hominum daemones esse in forma.' Took me awhile to figure out it was Latin and get a translation from the brain trust. I'm not so sure he was talking to me, though—might have been the other guy. With his gun still on the kidnapper, he pulled the trigger and painted the wall with the guy's brains and violet lead. Then, he didn't say shit, jumped through the window from the second floor and was nowhere to be found—nothing. Over the next few days, we discovered a total of six bodies, all female, in various locations on the property."

For a moment, Callaghan was silent. He repeated the foreign language phrase as Palmer had recounted, "I took some Latin in college—"

"Then you also know what it means."

"In life, devils exist in the forms of men."

The apartment grew quiet. Palmer moved to take a closer look behind the bar, while Callaghan began picking up the stools that had been disrupted during the struggle.

"Got something," Callaghan said.

Palmer maneuvered around the bar. "That makes you two for two now. What do we have?"

Charlie had taken a knee close to the bar. "It was underneath one of the stools." He then held a large black button aloft.

"One of these mob guys has a bad habit of losing buttons from a coat he probably can't afford."

"Either that..." Callaghan rose to his feet and dropped the button into Palmer's hand. "Or Mortuary killed Morgan Maxwell."

NINE

Tuesday, April 13, 1937.

THE CARDS LIKED TO PLAY the game his way. August Florian nodded his head in satisfaction as he spread a full house on the table for everyone to see.

"It's an allegory," Florian said.

Pete Aronstein was the only one who hadn't had the good sense to bow out when the hand had gotten hot. He threw his cards on the table face down. "A what?"

Florian addressed everyone at the table. "It means Chaplain is trying to show that unemployment and economic conditions aren't being helped by modern industrialization. He's saying that in a time where jobs are already hard to find for a lot of people, such efficiencies being developed are making it even more challenging."

Aronstein laughed. "That assembly line really kicked his ass, that's for sure."

Florian huddled his arms around the extensive collection of chips, hugging them toward him as the other four men at the table looked on in amusement.

"That's just what you need," Eddie Pierce chuckled as he swept up the cards for another hand. "Sometimes I just want to knock that little smirk off your face."

Most people in the circle knew him as Eddie Arson. Pierce was a prominent boxer in the early thirties, but his career was tanked when he ended up in prison for a small stint. The common joke was that he earned the nickname by burning down a barber shop after receiving a haircut he didn't like. The truth, however, was that it was his father's failing barber shop, and Eddie had conspired to set it ablaze so that his father could collect the insurance money and begin anew. During his time in prison, he was approached by August Florian, representing his employer, who had the offer to make Eddie in exchange for legal representation.

"Aw hell, Eddie. You know he'd sue you for assault. And then you'd just be adding to his little collection plate over there," Aronstein said.

Lenny Opherman swiped a napkin across his pencil mustache. He had been showing no mercy to the plate of food in front of him. Lenny hadn't even been dealt into the game yet on account of Eddie's previously public complaints regarding the cards being greasy. Lenny protested that one of the girls could sit on his lap and handle the cards again while he ate, but Pete Aronstein had caught him cheating the one and only time they allowed that to happen.

"I didn't like that he didn't talk," Lenny said.

Eddie bobbed his head, holding up a hand. "Who's that?"

"Chaplain." Lenny returned to the conversation. "Somebody should have told him the time for silent movies is over. They got this thing called talking now. What do you think, boss?"

Arturo Casadonte lowered his glass of whiskey and lit a cigarette. He had sat out of the game the last few hands. For him, the enjoyment came from just being around the table with some of his closest friends. Besides, it wouldn't have made him a very good host to take money out of the pockets of his companions and employees at his own place.

"I think if you keep eating like that, you're going to be outside running the block with Heavy Henry. Do you only eat when you come here?"

Lenny was the proverbial broom in the song about marriage. He already had another mouthful before he could answer, which he tried his best to maneuver around, much to everyone's discomfort. "No. I eat plenty when I ain't here, Mr. Casadonte."

"I think talking would have ruined the mystique," Casadonte said. "For him to do all those previous pictures the way he did and then change everything he had built—and what his fans were used to and expecting, just because the times have changed a little—well, it wouldn't have really been the Little Tramp character anymore. I doubt it would have been well-received."

Florian looked at Lenny. His cheeks were ballooned like a squirrel making room for storage. "Chaplain isn't the only one whose mystique would have been ruined by talking."

"Still better than ruining the cards," Eddie said, dealing another hand. "You in this time, Mr. Casadonte?"

Arturo flicked an ash into the ashtray, shaking his head. "I'm just here for the company."

Pete Aronstein looked at his cards, knowing he wasn't going to make himself a martyr this time around. "Did I tell you what Dicky Mason told me?"

"How is Dicky?" Lenny asked. "I haven't talked to him since he moved out west."

"He's good," Aronstein said. "He's throwing boxes on a pier now and loving the beach."

"Sounds like a nice little retirement to me." Florian gave no indication of his next winning hand. "That's where I'm going—the beach."

"Shit," Eddie countered. "You ain't going anyplace anytime soon. You just like your talk to be as big as your pockets."

Aronstein threw his ante into the pile. "So Dicky tells me that out west, there's this politician—"

"Which one?" Lenny asked.

"Jesus, Lenny—I don't know which one. Some small-time Democrat. You going to let me tell the story or not?"

Lenny Opherman stuffed his mouth again.

"This politician," Aronstein said, "He's supposed to be out doing public appearances—getting his name out there, promising free shit, you know? Well, he cuts his trip early and comes home to a house that ain't empty. Walks in his bedroom and what's he find?"

Florian answered, "His wife and his campaign manager pitching woo."

Pete Aronstein flipped his cards face down on the table, "Damn it, August—I can't just tell it how it goes?"

"That's what he found?" Casadonte asked.

Aronstein shook his head at Florian. "Yeah, that's what he found. This politician—his wife is smoking—that kind of gal that would make you get up singing in the morning. So this guy says the hell with that—pulls one of the rails from the banister of the stairs and proceeds to give his campaign manager an unforgettable shellacking. Wife calls the police—somehow they make it there before he kills the guy. Cops escort the politician out of the house and try to get this thing sorted out. One cop looks at the wife, then over to the campaign manager laying in buckets of his own blood and turns to his partner and says 'lucky guy.'"

The room filled with laughter.

"He didn't say that," Eddie doubted.

"That's what Dicky told me."

Florian held all his cards, declining to pick up more. "And how does Dicky know? Was he there?"

"I don't know." Aronstein shrugged. "That's just what Dicky told me."

"Okay." The joy faded from Arturo's tone. As much as he appreciated the moment, he hadn't been able to keep the prevalent thoughts in the back of his mind from rushing to the forefront without invitation. "We've got some other matters to discuss."

"Lucetti ain't going to play with us, is he?" Eddie shook his head.

"No." Casadonte closed his cigarette case and lit another. "I don't think he is. He's always been in Crocetti's back pocket, and he's putting me off while he waits to see where the chips fall."

Lucetti had wavered with fluidity over the years. As one of the underbosses, his allegiances had always remained foremost to Salvadore Barone, but it was the line between Casadonte and Crocetti that he regularly danced from one side to the other on. It was like he didn't want to bet on either horse until he saw which one had won the race.

"The will," Florian said. "He's waiting for Crocetti to collect whatever Mr. Barone left him."

Lenny finally finished his plate, pushing it to the side and wringing his hands on a cloth napkin. "I'm sorry for your loss, Mr. Casadonte."

"Yeah, we all are," Eddie said. "We know how close you and Mr. Barone were. And it's nothing but bullshit of the highest order that you can't go to his funeral—just because his brother-in-law is going to be there."

"You don't think the two of you can make nice?" Aronstein asked.

"He tried to kill me twice," Arturo said. "And if what happened at the docks didn't go down the way it did, we wouldn't have had to send Dicky to California in the first place. Am I supposed to be okay with that? Yeah, Nico, let's just forget about the time you shot up my car, and I pulled glass out of my ass for two weeks. Water under the bridge, old pal. Just don't shoot me in the back when I turn around."

Florian nodded in agreement, looking at Aronstein. "Yeah, I was there for that. And you know I don't carry a piece. I swear to God, I was scared out of my shit—I knew we were dead that night. If it hadn't been for Dicky..."

Eddie was genuinely concerned for the attorney. "How many times you been shot at, August?"

"Twice. That one was the first time, but it wasn't any kind of exercise in courage-building for when the second time came around, I'll tell you that."

"How about you, Eddie?" Lenny asked.

Eddie Pierce shrugged and wrinkled the corners of his mouth. "None. I never even seen a gun until I met you fellas."

Aronstein was in disbelief. "Really? So, no one ever made some threats—wanted you to fix a fight or anything? Show you their heater just to scare you?"

"You hear too many stories." Eddie laughed. "That don't happen in real life as much as you think it does."

"But you'd be scared, right?" Lenny Opherman had a habit of talking before he processed what it was he was saying—and in some cases—whom it was he was saying it to.

Eddie folded, pulling himself out of the game.

Casadonte had interjected before Eddie took Lenny's question the wrong way. "I imagine it's a little like boxing, Lenny, but with higher stakes. If you're not at least a little scared, you must not feel like you have anything to lose."

August spread his cards face-up, driving the chips in his direction while steering the conversation back on course. "So what are we going to do about Lucetti?"

"I'll set up a meeting," Casadonte said. "Pete and Eddie will go talk to him—see if we can get a line on some of that military hardware from Europe that he's been talking so much about."

Aronstein felt a hint of discomfort. "Boss, you sure you don't want August to go? Broker the deal instead? I mean, he's a better talker than me, and if things get heated, it's just going to end with Eddie punching people."

Eddie glanced to Pete in mock offense. It had never ended with Eddie punching people—although it had gotten close once or twice in the past. That was just another inaccurate assumption about a former boxer made on Aronstein's part. Shaking his head, he turned his attention back to Casadonte.

"Lucetti probably isn't going to sell us the weapons anyway. The point isn't to actually buy them—and it's certainly not for Eddie to punch people. You're gauging his demeanor, Pete. If he agrees to sell us the guns, then we'll know he's on our side. Or at least considering the possibility. And if he comes up with an excuse for why he can't sell—well, then we'll know he's already made his decision."

"Does that mean that I'm going somewhere with you, instead?" Florian asked.

"Yeah, just some legal mumbo jumbo I need you to be there to look at. I've got some papers to sign, but I want to make sure I know what I'm putting the pen to. To ensure I'm not—"

All four men at the table were startled by the sounds of a woman screaming in the main area of the club. Metal trays crashed raucously to the freshly waxed floor, and the other people out front began making a fuss. Everyone that was gathered around the table looked at one another.

Lenny reached into his coat the same time as everyone else, save Florian. "The hell?"

The door burst open, and the club's manager threw himself into the back room. His brow had gathered considerable perspiration, making his forehead even shinier than it normally was, and he tugged at the collar and bowtie dramatically, as if he were having trouble breathing. Aronstein was the one facing the door and had half-stood from his chair when it had unexpectedly flown open.

"I'm sorry, sir!" The manager was panting, looking around the room frantically. "I told him he would have to make an appointment. And then Heavy Henry said the same and he—I think he broke Henry's nose!"

The tall figure of Frank Palmer appeared in the doorway, rubbing the knuckles of his right fist.

Casadonte looked up, addressing the club manager. "Calm everyone down and get them back to the tables and the booze. And get one of the girls to see about Henry. I'll handle this."

The manager was ecstatic about taking his leave and Eddie, Pete and Lenny rose to their feet, hands itchy inside the folds of their jackets.

Arturo spread his arms, holding his hands out in an attempt to calm everyone down. "No."

"Fat guy out front didn't want to let me in," Palmer said.

The other men returned to their seats, under their employer's orders, but the ones with their chairs positioned facing away from the door remained turned toward Palmer, eyeing him suspiciously.

Arturo straightened the lapels of his coat and checked the top button before walking around the edge of the table toward the detective. As he approached, Casadonte opened his arms and wrapped them around Palmer in the way that someone would hug a brother.

"Mio Fratello."

TEN

Thursday, July 12, 1917.

THE WOMAN LOOKED down at him through pointy-edged glasses and turned her eyes back to the clipboard.

"Francis James Palmer—twelve years of age," She said flatly.

Nothing was inviting about the Crescent Ridge Children's Home. From the moment the car pulled up, Frank knew that the old foreboding structure was never going to feel like a home away from home. Even residing on a grassy hill that lay within the heart of the city, he wasn't able to tell that it hadn't been abandoned—or forgotten.

As he sat in the lobby waiting for his name to be called, Frank had noticed that the inside looked even worse. Paint peeled from the bland walls of white concrete, and he was pretty sure he saw mold on the ceiling, gathered heavily in one of the corners.

He looked around at the other kids in the lobby, which ranged from a few toddlers to older kids his age. Some of them looked to be in shock, some of them were crying, and one boy was just sitting there staring at the wall in front of him while kicking the leg of the chair with the back of his heel.

When the woman called his name, Frank answered. "Yes, ma'am. Francis J. Palmer."

"We have most of your records," the woman said. "First, you'll see the nurse, and she'll give you a basic check-up. Then, the doctor will make sure you've had the proper vaccinations."

"Okay?" Frank didn't intend for it to sound like a question. He glanced around the room again. It was a cold place in summer.

The woman put her hands on her hips, still holding the clipboard in one of them. "Because of your advanced age, you probably shouldn't be here, but due to your family circumstances, the state has insisted."

Where would he have gone otherwise? The streets? Part of him would have preferred that. Within thirty minutes of being at the children's home, Frank had already gathered what he felt would equate to a lifetime of resentment.

She continued, "Once the doctor is finished, you will report to me. I'll show you to your bunk."

"Yes ma'am," he said as another woman approached the first.

"I've got the first of this morning's batch squared away, Mrs. Ernestine," she said. "Do you want me to take any of these?"

"No, that's fine, Esther. I've only got two more and then they'll all be ready for the nurse."

"Going to be a busy next two weeks," the second woman said, smiling as she walked away. "There's a lot to do before the big day."

Frank watched as the woman with the pointed glasses moved on to the next of the kids. By the time she got to the fourth, he had memorized the routine. Verify your name, here's the spiel about the nurse and the doctor. If you're older than twelve, then you probably shouldn't be here, so you should be thankful life isn't any worse than sitting in the cold lobby of a ramshackle old building that was previously who knows what.

The fifteen minutes that followed seemed more like an hour. In the interim when no one was speaking, Frank heard the droning sounds of the clock nearby. At first, he would count along with the second hand but always lost interest before he could get to sixty.

At one point he heard the sounds of kids playing outside, so he got up to look through the window, but he wasn't able to see anything. They must have been on another side of the building.

Finally, a cute young nurse with brown hair made her appearance, smiling to him as he rested his elbows on the window, longing for the world beyond.

"Young Mr. Palmer?" She asked in a tone too jovial for anyone who had worked there an extended period of time.

"Yes ma'am, that's me."

"We're ready for your check-up now. Come with me?"

The nurse led Frank through a set of doors and down another long hallway. The further they got from the lobby, the more it smelled like medicine and alcohol. Some of the examination rooms were open—though the ones that were remained uninhabited as they passed.

The nurse made an attempt at small talk once they got into the examination room, shutting the door behind her.

"It says here that you're twelve. You're kind of tall for your age."

The preliminary exam went rather quickly, and the doctor arrived much sooner than Frank would have expected. The nurse assisted during the full exam, which involved checking his heart rate, his eyesight and whacking his knee with that funny little hammer.

Frank had removed his shirt and shoes as part of the procedure for measuring his weight and height. He wore a necklace of thin leather that attached to a pair of small circular aluminum pieces that dangled lifelessly in the air before pressing them close to his chest. He sensed he was being watched and turned to see the nurse's features soften as his eyes met hers just before she averted her gaze.

When he was reviewing the charts, the doctor had said, "Everything looks good, lad. You're in much better shape than many of the others who come through here."

"Why is that, sir?" Frank asked, pulling his shirt over his arms and buttoning the front.

"Past history—upbringing—things such as these are always a factor. What did your father do?"

As they conversed, the doctor was scribbling notes on various pages of Frank's documentation.

"He was a dentist."

The doctor nodded and closed the folder, patting Frank on the knee, smiling. "Well, I hate to make it sound like you're in jail, but don't worry, son. The time will pass quickly here, and you'll be out and into the world before you know it."

Once the doctor had left, the nurse smiled to Frank as he was putting his shoes back on.

"You know," she said, "That took about half the time it normally takes. They probably don't even have your bunk ready, yet. Why don't I take you down to the end of the wing and show you the exit so you can go outside and meet some of the other kids? I really don't think anyone would notice."

Shrugging, Frank finished tying his shoes and stood up, picking up his duffel bag and slinging it over his shoulder. It had been a long drive, and he wouldn't mind being able to stretch his legs for a while. He followed the nurse into the hallway and to the point where it finally ended. He could hear the sounds of kids outside.

"Okay," she said. "Fifteen minutes is probably enough time. Any more than that and Mrs. Ernestine may come looking for you."

Frank nodded and pushed the steel door open.

The morning air hit his face as a small boy nearly ran into him. The boy expertly navigated around Frank as if he were inanimate as he followed fast after his friend, giggles ringing into the schoolyard.

To his left were a row of see-saws and he instantly knew that wasn't going to be the side of the yard he would be exploring. Scanning the area for others his age, his attention was drawn to the sound of a girl yelling.

"Stop it!"

She was a pretty girl with brown curled hair, tied from back to top by a red ribbon. Frank guessed she was a year or two younger than he was. The source of her ire was a tall, hefty kid with a stick. He watched as the boy wagged the stick at the girl—presumably again—in an attempt to use it to lift her dress.

The girl turned to him again, clenching her fists. Cheeks reddened with the embarrassment of having one of her friends by her side, she screeched once more. "I said stop! If you don't, I'm going to tell my brother!"

"And what's he going to do?" The tall kid asked. "The last time someone tried to get in my face I hit him so hard that his broke like a car window. Pieces of his head just laying all over the ground."

She rolled her eyes and whirled away from him again, ignoring his bluster and returning to the attention of her friend. The boy started to poke the stick in her direction once more.

Frank called out to the kid. "Hey! Come on, now. How many times does she have to tell you?"

The boy turned to Frank, puffing his cheeks. "Just shut up and stand over there. That's all you're going to do anyway. You wouldn't want your pretty clothes to get all dirty, would you?"

His duffel bag fell from his shoulder and Frank began a brisk walk in a line directly to the boy. The girl's least-favorite annoyance raised the stick with one hand.

"You better watch yourself. I got this stick."

The kid never even had time to brandish it threateningly before Frank's fist connected with his mouth. He fell onto his back, dropping the stick and looking up with a shocked expression. The coppery taste informed him of the small trickle of blood that had formed in the left corner of his lips.

"Listen here, you son of a..."

Frank considered waiting for the kid to get up so he could hit him again.

"You can try to flip girls' dresses up, and you may be able to scare kids with your little threats. But if you've already made the mistake of thinking I'm going to be one of them—"

The kid held his mouth with both hands as he started to get up, tears forming in his eyes. "I'm going to tell!"

Frank shook his head. "Well, when you do, make sure you tell them the whole story, because if they ask me what happened, I'm just going to tell them that even if you had two asses to talk out of, I'd still kick them both."

Flush with embarrassment, the hefty kid tucked his tail and scampered away. He'd have to find smaller prey if he wanted to play predator anymore this morning.

Frank didn't realize that his fists were still tight, hands shaking, his fingernails cutting into his palms.

"Are you okay?" The girl asked. She was looking at Frank as though she couldn't believe what had just happened. She seemed leery of approaching too closely.

He then noticed that the rest of that side of the schoolyard was also looking in his direction. Frank relaxed his demeanor, loosening the muscles in his body.

"Yeah," he said. "I'm fine. Are you?"

Her curls bounced around the nape of her neck as she nodded, pulling downward on the folds of her blue dress and wringing it in her hands. "You're new, aren't you? What's your name?"

"Frank." Talking down a bully was easier somehow than standing before the girl with the dark hair and the red ribbon. He couldn't help but notice that her brown eyes were lovely, too.

On closer inspection, he realized that the girl's dress looked as though she wore it every day. It wasn't dirty, but she might have still been the third one to own it. A patch held one of the shoulders together, and there were tiny openings in each of the underarms where the seams were coming apart. Frank wouldn't know until later that it was one of the few that had been given to her by the children's home and was from one of the charity drives.

"Just Frank?" She asked, bringing a hand to her mouth in an imitation of shock. "Oh no, don't tell me they didn't even know your last name when they brought you here!"

It took a few seconds, but finally, the corner of his mouth curled and he almost laughed. "Frank Palmer."

The girl's arms went behind her back, offering a smile that made her eyes nearly disappear from squinting as she beamed, "Nice to meet you. I'm Cesca—Francesca Casadonte."

Cesca turned to the other girl, waving her closer. "And this is my friend, Hattie."

She was a little smaller than Cesca but appeared to be around the same age. She had short blonde hair that was tighter around her head. "Hi," she said, opening and closing her fingers with a shy wave.

"A pleasure, Hattie."

Cesca grabbed Frank's arm, tugging and nearly causing him to lose his balance. "You need to come with us. I want you to meet my brother. He's not going to believe what happened."

Frank centered his weight, making her stop. "Wait a minute. My bag."

After Frank had retrieved his duffel bag, she put her arm in his again and dragged him beyond the other side of the yard. When they were some distance away and clear of the others, the yard looked as though it would continue to stretch on forever. The property of the children's home was vast beyond the expanse of merely the building itself.

Cesca led Frank and Hattie down a hill and into an area where the trees and overgrowth began to get thicker. He could barely hear the sounds of the kids playing in the distance.

The group followed a trail until it rounded a corner where Cesca nearly ran over someone who was standing there. She seemed surprised, backing up to step all over the top of Frank's shoes, but not as surprised as the boy who wasn't expecting company.

The kid jumped with a start, fumbling a cigarette in his hands that dashed red sparks across the front of his jacket.

"Jesus, Cesca—you scared the hell out of me. I thought I was caught."

He was about Cesca and Hattie's age and sat on the largest tree stump Frank had ever seen. At one time it must have been a great monolith that had stood tall and unopposed, surveying everything around it. Now, though, it was a flat stump large enough for at least three people to comfortably sit on.

The fact that it was a smoking spot didn't seem to be a recent development, either. The top of the severed tree was marred by black spots where fire had been doused on its surface.

"Sorry," Cesca said. "I thought it was further along the trail than this." She put her arm in Frank's once more, pulling him forward. "This is Frank. He just got here this morning. And he wasn't in the yard for five minutes before he played Jack Dempsey on Chucky."

"What a jackass. Someone needed to." The kid held out his hand, but Frank had to pull himself away from the boy's sister to accept. "Arturo Casadonte. But you can call me Arthur if that sounds more American to you."

"Is that Italian?" Frank asked.

"Very good!" Francesca chimed.

"Anyone see you come out here?" Arturo asked his sister.

"I don't think so," she answered. "Do you want us to go back really quick and make sure?"

"Please," Arturo said. "I already thought you were going to be Mrs. Ernestine."

"Okay, we'll be back." Cesca ushered Hattie back toward the trail, turning her head to offer Frank a rosy-cheeked smile as they disappeared around the corner.

Arturo produced a ragged pack of cigarettes, lighting one of the bent ones. "She thinks I need to make friends." He held the pack out in offering, but Frank declined.

Moving over to the edge of the large stump, Arturo invited Frank to join him.

To Frank, Arturo and Cesca looked to be about the same age. "Are you twins?" He asked, joining Arturo on the spacious stump.

"Yeah, but she's prettier than me. I'm older by about four minutes, though." Arturo inhaled the cigarette and looked over to Frank. "So, since you're the new kid, I get to ask you how you got here."

He hadn't talked about it yet. The women at the children's home, the worker who came to pick him up— even the doctor and nurses who read his files—they already knew, so it had never come up for discussion.

"Come on. We're all going to find out eventually. You tell me, and I'll tell you. Deal?"

Arturo's clothes only looked to be on their second or third owner, but his shoes were barely holding together—especially the toes of the left one.

Frank leaned forward to pick up a small stone at the base of the tree trunk, shaking it around inside his hand as he spoke.

"My old man left to go to the war. We got a few letters from him, I think. One night my mom and I were on our way home and she just—broke down—I don't know. She was crying and holding the wheel so tight... She floored the pedal and next thing I knew—I swear—we must have been doing seventy down that winding road. I remember seeing headlights coming toward us and then I'm waking up, laying in the grass. The car was twisted like a melted piece of licorice, but she was still inside. I pulled her out, and I held her till the end before the police got there."

"Damn." Arturo shook his head, watching Frank toss the stone against one of the nearby trees. He leaned forward momentarily to make sure his sister wasn't back yet. "Our mom... She got telegrams from her family in Florence talking about how bad it was there. And one day we came home from school—she was just gone. Our dad got a message from her about a week later. Said she was going to get her parents out of there. That was the last we ever heard from her."

"What about your pops?" Frank asked.

"Went to go fight in Europe." He shook his head. "And the man who left Italy to find a better life went back there to die. How about yours?"

When Frank leaned down again to grab another rock, the necklace fell from inside his shirt.

Arturo used his cigarette as a pointing device. "What's that?"

"My dad's ID tags," Frank said, stuffing them back into his clothing. "From the war."

"You wear those things every day?" Arturo asked.

"Yeah, to remember him."

Arturo leaned back, putting his cigarette out in a spot that was already blackened. "You can remember what was lost without having to carry it around with you all the time. How much do those weigh?"

Frank tilted his head in confusion as he regarded Arturo. "Oh, they're aluminum."

"That's not what I'm asking."

This time, Arturo heard the crunching of leaves before someone rounded the corner. Cesca didn't have Hattie with her, and he threw up his arms, expecting news.

"They didn't see us come down here," Francesca said. "But Frank, a nurse is looking for you."

Frank bounded from the stump as though he had been sitting on ants. "Oh God—" He looked around to make sure he had possession of everything he had brought along. "I'm supposed to check back in!"

* * * * *

The last jolt nearly cut his head clean from his shoulders. Frank had to crane his neck back to keep her hand from hitting his chin when she put the finishing touches on his necktie. Finally, Mrs. Ernestine stepped back and admired her torturous handiwork with a nod of satisfaction.

Frank gave Arturo a sympathetic look as Mrs. Ernestine moved down the line to her next victim. It was his turn at the guillotine.

The boys were all lined up on one side of the hallway, backs to the wall, while the girls were similarly organized opposite them on the other wall. The starch in Frank's shirt made it a little itchy, but he hadn't been dressed as well since the last time he had gone to church.

There had been no expense spared in arranging everyone's attire. For the past two weeks, several tailors had made multiple trips to the children's home, taking measurements and holding fitting sessions.

Cesca was several girls down the line, but Frank's eyes kept meeting hers as the headmistresses went down the two rows. She looked so pretty in her new red dress and white tights, even from so far away, but to Frank, she may as well have been the only girl in the home. It even went perfectly with the ribbon she still insisted on wearing for such a momentous occasion.

No one had made him feel more welcome on his first day. She even covered for him when he was late in checking in, telling Mrs. Ernestine that Frank got lost wandering the halls of the building and that she found him and showed him where to go.

He wasn't sure whether or not he was supposed to be her boyfriend, but she sure acted like it.

"Dear God," Arturo said to Frank, tugging at the front of his collar with a finger. "This thing is killing me already. Whatever I end up doing after I get out of this place, you can bet it won't be wearing this kind of stuff except in rare circumstance."

"It's not that bad," Frank said. "The worst part for me is that it's the middle of summer."

"Maybe not for you—yours probably fits right. We don't even match. We're wearing black and gray, and the girls are all in red and white. Maybe a red vest or something—"

"Yours fits right, too. The five trips you made to the tailor to have it altered made sure of that."

Mrs. Ernestine clapped her hands, getting everyone's attention. "Okay, children. We're about to go out front. Our guest of honor will be here in a few minutes. Everyone is looking their best, and we've gone over the rehearsals enough that you all know what to do."

Arturo let his neck go limp so that the back of his head hit the concrete wall. "Yes, yes, we're going to make a good impression, lady."

Frank smirked. "The happiest poor little orphans you ever saw."

The girls filed down the hallway first and Cesca acknowledged Frank and Arturo as she passed. "I hope you remember the words," she said with a wry curl of her painted lips.

"Was she talking to you or me?" Arturo asked.

It was finally time for the boys' line to move. All dressed in black slacks, shoes, and jackets with gray vests, they followed behind the equally dapper girls.

Frank was surprised by the number of cars parked in front of the children's home. Both sides of the street were jam packed, though the circular driveway of the orphanage itself remained clear—presumably reserved for the esteemed guest.

The kids gathered outside on the front steps and formed their predetermined arrangement, creating a semicircle composed of separate gender lines on either side so that it expanded from the topmost area to the region where the car would be arriving.

The reporters had been waiting outside all morning at the bottom of the steps, and their impatience was satiated when the kids made their long-awaited appearance. Some of them began igniting flash bulbs.

There was space enough between the first boy and girl at the highest point to allow someone to walk between them. Mrs. Ernestine strode between that space and descended the front steps. When she reached the bottom, she paused and struck a pose, allowing the journalists to take a few photos with the children behind her.

Within the next few moments, Frank spotted four cars pulling onto the property. When Mrs. Ernestine noticed them, she demanded everyone's attention for the announcement.

"Okay, this is it. The entourage is arriving. Now remember, children—I will give the signal—but you have to begin the song the very second Mr. Barone steps out of the car."

The car came to a stop and a tall man of about fifty years rose majestically from the passenger side. As he did, Mrs. Ernestine gave the signal, and the orphanage's residents began their rehearsed song.

Salvadore Barone was wearing a black suit with a gray vest, along with a black bowler. He wore a pleasant smile and the sun reflected from a hand full of gold rings when he waved to the children. Moving faster than any of his escorts, Barone opened the door of the car that was parked behind his, and a lovely middle-aged blonde woman leaped from the car with exuberance, taking her husband's hand.

"How adorable," she said to him. "They're dressed just like us."

Salvadore had seen to the arrangements himself, having made sure that their ensemble was planned in advance and that the tailors would get it just right at the orphanage.

He smiled at his wife. "I thought you would appreciate that."

The two had to almost yell to be heard over the melodious tone of the children's song. Salvadore took her arm in his and escorted her to the steps. Several of his men exited the four vehicles and moved silently along with them.

The couple ascended the front steps of the children's home as the song continued. Mrs. Barone smiled to each girl as she passed and Salvadore kept catching the flash of the cameras in the corner of his eye. With each kid they passed, the two columns of youth turned with the couple so that they were facing the opposite direction, toward the top of the stairs.

When they had reached the top, Salvadore nodded to Mrs. Ernestine while his wife took the headmistress's hand in hers and he turned to face the group of youngsters. The echo of the song faded as he applauded them heartily.

"Thank you, children. It is an honor to be here today. First, I'd like to thank Mrs. Ernestine for making this all possible…"

Salvadore also addressed the press. "As you all know, I have a great, open heart. Whenever an opportunity for charity arises, it pulls at the strings inside. I couldn't think of a better reason to be here today than the eyes of the young people I see before me at this moment. Many of them are here because of the sacrifices their fathers have made." He thrust a pointed finger into the air several times. "A sacrifice that has continued to preserve freedom and keep not only this country—but the world—safe from the German scourge. A sacrifice that cannot be allowed to be forgotten by those of us who have the ability to do something about it."

Everyone in attendance applauded, and Salvadore held up his hands, noting that he was not finished with his speech.

"It is why I'm here today. I would like to announce that I am making a donation—in the sum of ten thousand dollars—to the boys and girls of the Crescent Ridge Children's Home. No longer will they not be privy to the semblance of a somewhat normal life during a time that has made almost everything for them abnormal."

The cameras flashed as everyone cheered. Salvadore shook Mrs. Ernestine's hand politely, and both of them turned to smile for the cameras as he still held her hand in his.

"Let's get some of you and the children," she said.

"A fantastic idea, dear lady," he replied, stretching his arms wide over the group as though he were going to hug them all at once.

The children all moved to the top of the stairs and gathered around the guest of honor. Salvadore pointed to Frank and Arturo. "I want these two here beside me. And let's get a girl, too."

"Sir, that's my sister over there," Arturo said, pointing to Francesca.

"Yes, that will be perfect." Salvadore reached out to his wife. "Come stand with me, dear."

The group scrunched together and got as organized possible, with Salvadore on the left and his wife on the right. Frank and Arturo were on the outside of Salvadore and Cesca was opposite Mrs. Barone. Mrs. Ernestine had seen fit to position herself directly behind the happy couple.

Maybe one of the papers had managed to get a photo of the entire group with everyone's eyes open at the same time.

"Okay," Salvadore said happily. "I think that will be enough. Thank you, everyone."

The conglomeration broke, and everyone began to separate, spreading across the front yard of the children's home, talking among themselves.

Cesca smiled at Frank and crossed over toward him as Salvadore turned to join his wife and Mrs. Ernestine in their tour of the children's home so he could see the dilapidation for himself.

The gleam of something that wasn't a camera caught Frank's attention and he pushed Cesca aside with one arm and pressed his knee into the back of Salvadore's leg, causing the man to go down onto the concrete.

Gunfire echoed through the property.

The reporters either dove to the ground or ran for cover behind one of the vehicles that were parked on the side of the road. Barone's men already had their weapons drawn and were firing back across the street—the reporters caught in the crossfire.

Instantly, chaos had erupted on the front lawn, and the kids were screaming and running for their lives—most of them toward the front doors of the children's home as the headmistresses ushered the panic-stricken youngsters from harm's intent.

Whirling to grab Cesca, Frank hugged her closely and took her down on top of him to cushion her fall, immediately rolling over so that he lay atop her. She was on her side covering her head with her arms, eyes clenched shut. He gathered his own arms to further shield her upper body so that her head was near his shoulder.

When Frank looked up to see what was happening, Mrs. Barone was lying on the ground; a pool of red tendrils had begun spreading out from around her body. Arturo was kneeling beside her, holding her shoulder with both his hands. Somehow, he was covered in blood as well, but he didn't look like he had been hit.

He was a sitting duck—Arturo made a lone target in the middle of a shooting gallery. Bullets struck the sign nearby and threw concrete dust into his face as they ricocheted off the ground, but he didn't move, nor did he loosen his grip on the wounded woman.

Salvadore Barone had remained on the ground. His men dutifully stood between their employer and the danger that was clearly meant for him. They continued shooting as tires squealed and a black car sped away, vanishing from the scene.

An older man burst from the orphanage doors, hurrying toward the group. He stopped in his tracks when he saw the woman lying in blood and turned to Salvadore. "I'm a doctor, sir. We need to get her inside—now."

Salvadore couldn't speak. It was all he could do to nod his head. He tapped one of his men with the back of his hand as he rose slowly to his feet, unable to remove his gaze from his wounded wife.

The boy at her side wore the woman's blood across the front of his vest and jacket, though it could hardly be seen on the dark material of the coat. Arturo slid back to allow the doctor and two of Barone's men to be able to move her.

Salvadore looked on silently as his wife was carried toward the orphanage's main structure.

Frank and Cesca were on their feet. Tears stained her cheeks as he hugged her tight against him. "It's okay—it's okay," he said. "As long as I'm around, I'll never let anything hurt you."

Eyes affixed on the doors, Barone only stared straight ahead while he addressed Arturo. "You know that's my wife."

The adrenaline was fading from Arturo's body, and his hands had begun to shake. "Y—yes sir, I know."

"What's your name, son?"

"Arturo Casadonte, sir."

"You probably kept her from bleeding out." He still hadn't turned his eyes to Arturo. "Might have saved her life. You're the one with the sister, right?"

Arturo nodded. His knees were trembling, and the blood on his clothing had grown cold. For a moment, he thought he might throw up. "Yes, sir—we took the pictures."

Salvadore finally drew a deep breath, straightening his necktie and pulling the knot securely. "You and your sister will be well taken care of for the rest of the time you are here. My people will make sure that you never want for anything. Same for the kid who knocked me down."

His sister was still undergoing much-needed consolation, so Arturo looked back up to Salvadore. "That's Frank Palmer, sir."

"Good. And one more thing, Arturo. When you do leave here in a few years... I want you to come find me. I'll have a job for you."

Barone then began the long walk toward an uncertain future.

ELEVEN

Tuesday, April 13, 1937.

THE BACK ROOM of the club had been emptied almost immediately. While the others were cautious of leaving the detective alone with their employer, August Florian shook Palmer's hand on the way out.

"How is the Buick working out for you?" He had asked.

"I like it," Palmer said. "My partner was awestruck by the radio."

Florian looked confused.

"He's a rookie," Frank explained.

On his way out the door, Eddie had given Arturo a concerned look, as if to say that Casadonte should just yell if he needed him.

With the room clear, the two men looked across the table to one another, and Arturo knew such a thing wouldn't be necessary.

"It's been awhile. Haven't seen you since Florida," Arturo said.

"Yeah," Palmer replied. "Work. You know."

"Well, the first thing I'm going to have to ask is to what circumstance do I owe the pleasure?"

Casadonte leaned back in his chair and retrieved a cigarette from the case. He offered it to Palmer, who gladly accepted.

Palmer lit the cigarette and put the lighter back into his coat pocket. "Morgan Maxwell."

Blowing smoke into the air, Arturo nodded. "Yeah, I heard about that. Wait—you don't think I had something to do with that, do you?"

"Your name came up when we were asking some initial questions about the ordeal. And I know he owed you money. Thought it might be a possibility."

Arturo made a gesture that indicated that he wasn't completely in the know.

"How much did he owe me?"

"Hard to say," Palmer admitted. "We have some of his ledger books, but they're coded. Pretty simple stuff, but I didn't waste a lot of time trying to figure it out."

"Well," Casadonte said. "If I don't even remember how much it is, then I guess it wasn't worth killing the sap over."

Palmer shrugged, finding himself rather satisfied with that explanation. He never suspected that Arturo would have killed Maxwell, but even if he had, there would have been a better reason than that.

"Do you know Roselyn Farrell?" Frank asked.

Casadonte grinned as if he recalled fond memories.

"Sure I do. She's a lot of fun to be around, that one. I know Emma really likes her." Arturo then realized that something might be wrong. "She's okay, though, right?"

Palmer nodded. "A couple guys showed up at her apartment asking about Maxwell. They roughed her up a little, but nothing too serious. Luckily for her, a third party showed up. I'm looking for two guys—one of them short and fat and the other tall and skinny. They took a beating from said third party, so they'll be noticeably marked."

"I only have one beat up guy," Arturo laughed. "And apparently you did that."

Casadonte poured himself a drink. He held the bottle up as if asking Frank if he wanted one as well, but Frank waved it away.

"Want me to let you know if I hear anything? I can put some ears to the ground for you."

"Yeah," Palmer said. "That could help. But really, if you're off the list, then I'm pretty sure it's going to be Crocetti."

"I'll see what I can find out." Arturo assumed the business part of the discussion was over, so he decided to change the subject. "You still got that little gun you named after your dog?"

"The bite is just as bad as the bark," Palmer said.

Arturo laughed. He had fond memories of the past few years that he had spent with his friends—August, Eddie and the others, but it just wasn't the same as a reunion with someone he had grown up with.

"But what if someone comes at you with superior firepower and all you have is that little six-shooter?"

"I usually keep a shotgun in the trunk," Palmer said flatly. "But if I can't get to it, then Maurice will be great for getting a better gun with."

"Speaking of six-shooters," Casadonte said. "Do you still collect those old cowboy dime novels and magazines that you were so into when we were kids?"

He did. Frank had built up quite the collection during the past twenty years. Some of them required extensive travel, but most of them were mail-ordered to him after he put ads in several papers in the surrounding areas. A number of them had been destroyed since the times of their printing, but a few of the publishers sometimes had some on hand—especially if they were twentieth-century publishers. The others he typically purchased from private individuals.

"I've got a shelf full of them now," Palmer said. "I've got a Billy the Kid from the late 1800s. That's probably the best one in the arsenal."

"I bet you paid more than a dime for it," Arturo mused. "You always wanted to be like Aston Glass. Hey, what was it the Indians called him again? Oh yeah— Severed Eagle, right? And Cesca was Autumn, and I was— what was his name?"

"Remington Helm," Frank said. If the three of them were going to be a gang, that was a good one to be.

"That's him. I always thought it was ironically fitting that your name is Frank James, so I didn't understand why we couldn't have just been the James Gang."

"Because the James Gang didn't have any girls in it. And I wasn't going to leave her out."

Arturo peered into his glass, frowning. His change in expression indicated that he was already aware of the inevitability of her name coming up in the conversation at some point. He hadn't seen Frank in almost two years, and that wasn't the type of thing they were going to be able to avoid talking about when they saw one another again—even if it had been twenty years.

"Coming up on two years pretty soon," Arturo said, attempting a tone slightly above longing. "I was going to reach out before September. See if you wanted to come with me."

"What the hell for?" Palmer asked. "It's empty—there's nothing there, Arthur—just a headstone with some words on it."

Arturo's reactionary expression was an amalgamation of disbelief and chagrin. He paused and forcefully put his cigarette out in the ashtray.

"Did you really just say that?"

"I'm sorry," Palmer said, sighing. "I just..."

His voice trailed off.

"I loved her, too. She was my sister—my *twin* sister—I know she was the entire world to you, and God knows—I'd be devastated if anything ever happened to Emma, but she was a part of me forever. Having that piece lost is something I'm never getting back, either."

Frank looked to the side, unable to make eye contact. He had never talked about it with anyone. Not when it happened and certainly not with anyone at work. Most of them knew, but they avoided the discussion entirely—until long beyond the time for condolences to have been relevant.

"I should have just dropped that Goddamned case and gone with her like we planned."

Arturo sat back in judgment; he could sense what Frank was feeling. The man had never even allowed himself time to properly grieve. Somehow he blamed himself, and it had been burning away at him for nearly two years.

"The God's Acre Murders? That was *incasinato*, Frank." He clarified when Frank struggled to translate from Italian. "Messed up. You couldn't have known what was going to happen."

"I should have been there."

Arturo shook his head in disagreement. "And tell me, what were you supposed to do against a hurricane?"

"Nothing," Frank said. "But whatever happened, we would be together right now. She wouldn't have been there all alone—and I wouldn't be here alone."

Arturo poured himself another drink.

Frank turned back to him. "A train gets derailed—eleven cars ripped from the tracks—and everyone on the train survives..."

Choking on his words, Palmer summoned the reserves of his will, drawing it from behind eyes of misty glass.

"For God's sake... They never even found her."

Frank and Arturo had done everything they could in Florida following the Labor Day Hurricane of 1935. They joined the search parties and for three weeks they scoured the destruction in search of those who survived—and for those who didn't. Signs were even posted offering a reward to anyone who found Francesca—in any condition—a reward initiated and backed by Salvadore Barone himself.

"And when twelve years of marriage is suddenly gone—" Frank sighed. "Sometimes I still don't know what to do with myself."

"What about the job?" Arturo asked.

"It used to matter. Now I'm just grateful for having it so that it takes up the majority of my time."

Casadonte offered Frank another cigarette, snapping the gold case closed and tossing it on the table.

"Do you remember why you became a cop in the first place?" Arturo asked.

Frank shrugged. "So I could wear a uniform—be a little like our old men, I guess."

"Then why didn't you just join the army?" Arturo asked.

"No war to fight," Frank said. "But now... There's been this anger. It's getting real hard to suppress. And I want to take it out on someone."

"Don't you get to beat up bad guys sometimes? Hey, you know Eddie Pierce, right?"

"Yeah," Frank replied. "Big guy who was just in here giving me the eye. He used to be a boxer, didn't he?"

Casadonte threw back his glass of whiskey and cleared his throat.

"He owns a gym over on Central. Why don't you go by there sometime and beat the hell out of some heavy bags? Maybe even get in the ring and go a few rounds with one of the guys. Might help you blow off some steam."

Frank considered the possibility. It might be therapeutic in a way. But he knew he wasn't going to be getting in the ring with Pierce if he could help it.

"That's what I did when I heard about Salvadore," Arturo said, attempting to submerge his dejection.

Frank took a breath and looked up at him.

"That's the same night Maxwell was killed, too. I haven't talked to Sal for the last few years—figured it would be best to steer as far as possible after I made that little business go away."

"Sal never even asked you to do that. But he always said for me to tell you how much he wanted to thank you."

Frank shook his head. "After all he did for us when we were at Crescent Ridge? It was the least I could do for the father the three of us had when we needed one the most."

"Look, Frank," Arturo said. "It was only a matter of time before we saw each other again and had this conversation. I know you've been doing your own thing lately and that because of our particular—circumstances— sure, we have to be careful about being seen together, but two years?"

"You're right. We should do something," Frank said as he picked up his hat from the table and started to rise.

"I'm going to the matches Thursday night. Want to come watch some heavyweights go at it?"

"Pierce isn't fighting again, is he?"

"No," Arturo laughed. "Eddie is blacklisted for life. Besides, I'm talking wrestling, not boxing."

Frank gave the idea some consideration. It might be good for him to get out and do something for a change. This reunion with Arturo was the ice that needed to be broken and with the matches starting so late, it was unlikely they would be seen together. Besides, it was easy to get lost in the crowd.

Frank grinned, situating his hat atop his head. "So, tell me: is Dean Detton still the World Heavyweight Champion?"

Casadonte appeared to take that as a sign of Frank's acquiescence, which seemed to relieve him, and Arturo grabbed his cigarette case, standing up and donning his own hat as well.

"He damn sure is. I'm leaving too, so I'll walk out with you. I have an early morning with some lawyers, so I'm just going to leave this bunch of yahoos to it. And considering you probably scared the hell out of everyone out front, I don't want there to be any more trouble on your way out."

The activities in the front area of the club didn't seem to have missed a beat. The action at the tables was still going strong, and the bar was packed.

One of the girls was at the bar, tending to Henry's nose. He had tissue stuffed in each nostril, and the front of his face was swollen. When he saw Frank, Henry came off the stool.

"You son of a—"

Eddie stepped in front of Henry, leveling an arm as though it were a toll gate.

When Casadonte and Palmer reached the group, Arturo regarded Henry. "It's okay, he's with me."

"Well somebody could have told me that!" Henry yelled.

"I did tell you that," Frank said. "But I get it—your mistake—you didn't know any better."

Henry gritted his teeth and started to say something else, but the look Casadonte gave him put the big man back on the stool.

"Besides," Arturo said to Henry, "You've got a pretty lady taking care of you. Enjoy it."

Once Eddie was convinced that Henry was going to be suitably calm long enough for Palmer to get out of the building, he joined August, Lenny, and Pete as they gathered around their employer.

"Don't forget you're with me in the morning," Arturo said to August. "Pete and Eddie, you handle the meeting just like we talked about. We'll get together at my office afterward."

"You want me to drive you, boss?" Lenny asked.

"No, I'll handle it. You fellas play some more cards or something and have a good time. Everybody looks pretty calm, so make sure it stays that way."

The men nodded their understanding and Florian shook Palmer's hand again before they departed.

The street out front was quiet, despite the sounds of merriment within.

Casadonte was looking for his car parked across the road when his eyes fell directly upon three men getting out of the one parked behind his. Each of the men was followed by a long rifle with a wooden stock and steel barrel that he drew from within the confines of the vehicle.

"Oh shit. Frank..."

Palmer saw the men and went to draw his pistol, but wasn't fast enough to do so before they opened fire. Automatic weaponry sawed across the top of the car Palmer dove behind. He looked over to see that Casadonte was still standing there, getting ready to return shots with the .45 he had summoned from inside his coat.

Frank cursed and dashed across the club's front patio again, lowering his head and tackling Casadonte at the waist. Palmer dragged him by his coat until they were both behind cover, leaning against the side of another vehicle.

Glass rained down upon the two men as bullets ripped into other side of the car like wet cardboard.

"What the hell?" Casadonte was almost breathless. "Jesus, I thought those were shotguns!"

TWELVE

THE SILENCE WAS ABRUPTLY shattered by the discordant notes of death. Palmer pressed himself against the car and waited for an opening to present itself.

"MP18s!" He yelled to the man beside him. "Those were made for fighting in trenches. We're going to get slaughtered if we don't start shooting back."

"Thanks for clearing that up."

Maurice was warm in his hand, and Palmer raised up to fire a shot over the hood of the car before returning to his position of cover.

"I'm getting pretty good at protecting mobsters," Frank said.

Arturo pulled the slide and chambered a round. "I hope you stay good at it."

Palmer took another breath that he thought was extremely loud at first until he realized that the sound he heard was the air releasing from one of the punctured tires on the other side of the car.

"My boys will be out here in a minute, I hope," Casadonte said. "But in the meantime... I'm as ready as I'm going to be."

Arturo rose and squeezed the trigger twice. He was pretty sure that both shots hit the car the attackers were ducking behind.

The next time Frank fired off two shots, and he saw one of the men go down.

"I think I hit one of them in the arm," Frank said.

Palmer and Casadonte fired twice more each, but with no positive results.

"I'm going to have to reload in a minute," Frank said. "You're going to have to hold—"

The light from across the street gave the man away, casting his shadow on the concrete at Frank's side. The attacker had intended to sneak around the side of the car and mow them down with his machine gun in one swift stroke.

Instead, Palmer whirled around the edge of the car and released his last bullet into the man's chest. He dropped the MP18 and Frank caught it before it hit the ground. Ducking back behind the car again, Palmer rose above the hood and held the trigger.

Frank had never fired an automatic weapon before. It didn't have the recoil he was expecting and just squeezing the trigger for a second set off a burst of about eight or so rounds. He didn't hit any of their attackers, but the windows in the car they were using as cover were never going to cause any trouble again.

A second automobile rounded the corner and squealed to a stop in the middle of the street, producing four more men with similar armaments.

Arturo expressed a sigh of relief when the other four men—everyone but Florian—spilled from the front of the club, taking post a few cars down from them.

"I think we have five of them now," Palmer said.

Casadonte made a gesture to the other three, opening his hand widely to show all five fingers. Eddie nodded and squeezed off a few shots at the assailants.

When Palmer pulled the trigger again, he was more accustomed to the weapon's handling and thunder followed the lightning. One of the men in the distance received a diagonal strip up his chest from bottom to top.

Pete Aronstein was pointing toward the door of the club. Palmer nodded and gave him a signal.

"Look," Frank said to Arturo. "We can handle this. I'm going to cover you, but you need to make a break for the door. If we can get you out of here, then these guys will probably back off."

Nodding, Arturo thrust another clip into his pistol.

"Wait until I shoot," Frank said.

Then, Palmer ran to the next car down the line, staying low. Gunfire followed his trail, but he was safe for the moment. He paused to allow time for the bullets to rend the other end of the car. He wasn't dumb enough to try to move that much at once. They would have to do better than that.

Raising up again, Frank unleashed more fire from the MP18 machinegun. He looked at Arturo, who was waiting for the signal, but Palmer waved his arm in a straight line, indicating that it wasn't time to move yet.

Meanwhile, Casadonte's boys continued to let the lead fly. Palmer wasn't sure if they were hitting anything, though or if they were just trying to cover for the moment when Arturo made his move.

Palmer scrambled to the next car. This time, he had to take a dive to keep from being ripped apart. He rolled hard on the asphalt, tearing the elbow of his coat— probably some of the skin underneath, too—but the adrenaline was going strong now, and he didn't feel a thing.

When he looked back to give Eddie the signal, Palmer saw that he had lost his hat somewhere along the way. It lay directly in the line of fire, now full of holes. Frank couldn't see Eddie in the dark from so far away, so he waved and hoped for the best before popping up over the trunk of the car that was a makeshift shelter from a storm of lead.

Expending the remainder of the rounds in the weapon's drum, Palmer wasn't aiming for anything in particular—he just wanted to keep Arturo from getting cut down on his way back to the club. The other four men followed his lead, firing away with pistols and shotguns.

Frank ducked back down and tossed the smoking MP18 aside, drawing Maurice again and emptying the cylinder. He pushed six more rounds in with a sense of urgency while he looked for Arturo. The mob boss was nowhere to be found.

Before Frank could close the cylinder, one of the attackers rounded the corner and leveled his machine gun at the detective. Palmer would never get to the man's weapon in time.

Crimson ichor was jettisoned across the car window, and the man's knees went limp. He dropped to the ground like a puppet that a child was suddenly finished playing with and had cast aside.

The shot had come from above.

Palmer looked upward to see a black figure on the rooftop behind him, on the building next to the club. The shadowy form held a pair of Colt 1911 pistols—one of them casting the grayish white breath of the reaper into the night air.

Grabbing the machinegun that lay beside the fallen would-be killer, Palmer sent it skidding across the ground toward Aronstein and the others. The weapon made it close enough that one of them was likely to be able to reach it.

By Frank's calculations, there were—at most—three of the hit squad left, plus the one he thought he hit in the arm, who probably wasn't in good enough shape to be fighting right now. Arturo was safely inside, and his four men could probably handle it from here.

That was Mortuary on top of that building.

Crouching low, Palmer kept his head down as he deftly made a break for the alley. No shots followed him, and he was out of sight in an instant. When he was clear, Frank was able to move at full speed and leaped toward the fire escape.

His foot slipped, and he lost his grip for a moment—just long enough for one of the rungs of the fire escape to catch him underneath the ribs. It was sufficient to knock the wind from his lungs, but Palmer filled his body with much-needed oxygen as he resumed his ascent.

Holding his breath until he reached the rooftop, he scrambled over the ledge and brought his hand to his side. Hunched over, he finally exhaled and scanned the area for signs of his elusive quarry.

He had made it to the top just in time to see the shrouded figure on the other side of the building, leaping onto the next one with a panache that only backed up Frank's guess that it wasn't something Mortuary was unaccustomed to.

The hint of burning coal permeated the air above the roof, and Palmer drew deep of the acrid atmosphere before bounding across the rooftop in pursuit. He cursed his lack of physical regimen. It has been months since he'd chased a suspect on foot, and even longer since he'd done much of anything that could be interpreted as regular exercise.

Palmer skidded to a stop on the loose gravel mere feet before he reached the edge of the building. The dim lighting had made it impossible to measure the distance, but he then saw he could have made the jump with minimal effort. He clenched his fist and struck at nothing in the air. Damn it, why did he have to think about the ramifications of not making the jump? And why did he have to look down? Turning, he jogged a few paces in the opposite direction from the ledge and made a second attempt.

With his heart already pumping in his ears, he soared across to the other side with plenty of room to spare. Then, Palmer ripped the coat from his shoulders to reduce his carried weight, losing none of his momentum in the process.

It was just like the incident with Jackie Stockton.

The bicycle had been a few years old and was a gift from the Howell family once their youngest son had outgrown it, which was a hand-down from their eldest son, to be sure. It wore a thin coat of rust like armor that gave the bicycle an aged look—as though the collected wisdom of riders past could be imparted upon a new proprietor.

And it became Frank's most prized possession. With a pair of wheels and a simple metal frame, he could get anywhere in the neighborhood near the Crescent Ridge Children's Home twice as fast.

He rode the bicycle everywhere and sometimes nowhere, as riding in circles around the girls his age—especially Cesca—impressed upon them an eligible young shark who could leave the shallow waters at any time and ride into the deep asphalt ocean with an exhilaration of freedom.

So when Frank came outside to find the bicycle missing one day, he was immediately overcome with the anxious possibility that his means of two-wheeled freedom had been lost.

That was when he saw Jackie Stockton riding away on his bicycle. It didn't happen that way, but Frank always remembered Jackie cackling into the air like a matinee villain who had just pulled off his master plan without a hitch.

Before he had time to think, Frank's legs were pumping, and he was hot on Jackie's trail as fast as they would carry him.

Jackie spotted Frank and took a left turn, pedaling faster when he noticed that the bicycle's owner was in pursuit.

Running as hard as he could, Frank rounded the corner a few seconds after Jackie had. He was beginning to tire, and there was no way he was ever going to be able to catch up with the bicycle. Frank stopped running, breathing heavily, almost ready to throw in the towel.

Seeing a loose piece of concrete at the edge of the sidewalk, Frank snatched it up and hurled it as hard as he could in Jackie's direction.

Miraculously, the chunk of concrete nailed Jackie on the upper back, directly between the shoulder blades. The boy twisted the handlebars, losing control and both bicycle and rider lurched and went back-over-front into the air.

As Frank remembered it, the bike landed on Jackie's face, and he was crying when Frank finally reached him. He felt the same urge he had with the fat kid trying to lift Cesca's dress that day—he wanted to punch him as soon as he stood up.

Instead, Frank picked up the bicycle and hopped on, riding away feeling like the conquering hero who had thwarted the villain's master plan.

Currently, he was losing sight of Mortuary in the darkness. It wouldn't be much farther before the black figure was out of sight.

Palmer paused when he reached a brick chimney, examining it curiously. Reaching for one of the bricks on the outer edge, he was able to loosen it from the aged cement that had once held it soundly.

A shot rang out, hitting the chimney, only three feet from where he stood. The impact of the bullet split the brick and cement, scattering pieces across Palmer's slacks.

It was never going to be that easy.

Frank dropped the piece of brick and reached into his coat, baring the teeth of his favorite dog.

The gunshot came from behind him, so he knew it couldn't be Mortuary. Palmer jogged across the rooftop and slid on the side of one leg, scattering the gravel beneath him until he ended up behind the chimney, hoping that the brick structure would be able to survive another few shots if it came to that.

Narrowing his eyes, Frank tried to make out signs of the shooter in the distance. At first, he didn't see anything, but then he noticed a man rise from behind the ledge on the other building, squeezing off another round.

It had to be one of those guys who were trying to take out Casadonte.

There was no way he was going to be able to get a clear shot from so far away. One of them was going to have to close, and the other man probably wasn't at a disadvantage in the darkness.

He stayed low and crept across the gravel surface of the building. The shooter rose and fired again, but the bullet came nowhere close. Within seconds, Frank was behind the ventilation system, which would make better cover than a chimney that was already falling apart.

Sparks flew from the metal on the edge of the vents and Palmer pivoted around the corner to fire off a shot of his own in return.

He still needed to get closer.

A shootout in the dark is a sure way to get killed.

Frank went around the other side of the ventilation system just in time to see the man make the leap from the adjacent roof to the one Palmer currently occupied. Their eyes met for an instant.

Palmer fired first. The bullet hit the man in the neck and sent him sprawling backward, until at last, his large form toppled backward over the ledge.

Palmer ran to the edge of the building to look down, unsurprised by what he found there. The man was twisted—his limbs stretched in all directions—on the ground forty feet below—dead for sure.

The familiar and resounding sound of a hammer being pulled back—twice—urged Frank to slowly turn from the ledge.

Mortuary stood not twenty feet from him—both pistols leveled and ready to fire at the slightest infraction.

THIRTEEN

AIDED BY THE LIGHT of the moon above, Palmer was able to see Mortuary more clearly than he had during their previous encounter.

Everything was exactly as he remembered it.

The mask with the round dark eyes that reminded him of a gas mask, the hat that Roselyn Farrell said never fell off his head, the long black coat—and of course—the two Colt 1911 pistols, which were currently aimed in his direction. He felt a lot better when it was a babbling scientist guilty of murder instead.

Frank held his .38 high and pointed upward, with his finger away from the trigger, making sure the man before him did not feel threatened.

"Want me to drop it?" Palmer asked.

The black hat moved slowly from side to side.

"I want you to put it away," Mortuary said.

The voice hadn't changed, either. It was like a radio station that wasn't getting good reception—not difficult to understand but resonating over the layer of static that the sound rode on top of.

"Slowly," the radio-like voice instructed.

Making no sudden movements, Palmer returned Maurice to the holster inside his coat and revealed his empty hands as a sign that he had no ill intent.

Mortuary lowered his weapons and also made them disappear inside his coat, pulling it tight around his chest.

"Why are you following me?"

"I might ask you the same thing," Palmer said.

For what seemed like an eternity, neither man spoke. A hundred questions danced through Frank's mind, but he couldn't bring himself to make a decision as to which one to ask.

He decided to go with the first one that he had thought of.

"That's a nice coat. You're a Bankston Brower man, I see. Did you kill Morgan Maxwell?" Palmer asked.

"No."

"Do you know who did?"

"Not yet," Mortuary said.

It was impossible to read someone who had no facial expressions—no eyes to look into—and the man's body language seemed relaxed, but more in the way that a spring was relaxed when coiled. There was no way to tell what he was thinking or what he may do next.

"What were you doing at Roselyn Farrell's apartment the night she was attacked?"

"I followed you there. Two men were watching you leave. So I tailed them when they left and when they came back."

"But I was there that morning," Palmer said.

Mortuary gestured to his own clothing.

"I do not wear this all the time," he stated. "Those men—Benny Cassano and Joey Donati—I've learned since then that they work for Nico Crocetti."

"I figured as much," Palmer said. "But I still want to know why you followed me."

"It was not the first time," Mortuary said.

"Kind of like tonight?" Palmer asked. "And why would a guy trying to do a hit on Casadonte follow me up here?"

"They weren't trying to kill Casadonte."

"What the hell does that mean?" Palmer asked.

"They arrived just after you did and waited the entire time for you to come out of the club. I can only surmise that they tailed your car."

That didn't make any sense. If those guys worked for Crocetti and Barone was out of the picture, then what did a shootout in front of Casadonte's club have to do with Frank?

"They had MP18s," Frank said.

"I know."

"We found a warehouse with a few crates of those a couple months back. We couldn't prove it, but what we do know most likely leads the guns back to Gyp Lucetti."

Lucetti was a small-time player. He would have had even less reason to want Frank dead. Their paths had never even really crossed.

Right now he needed to focus on Crocetti.

"You think that's who killed Maxwell? Someone working for Crocetti? Maxwell owed him a boatload more than any of the other families."

"And you would know this," Mortuary stated.

I can't see your face, but you're a smug son of a bitch, aren't you?

"Meaning?" Palmer made no effort to hide those thoughts from his expression.

"You were at the club of a known criminal. You walked through the front door with him. When gunfire was exchanged, you made sure he was out of harm's way before making your next move. Just because you are friends doesn't necessarily mean you are in his pocket, does it?"

Palmer's fist closed tightly.

"You trying to rattle my cage?" He asked.

"No," Mortuary said. "It was merely an observation. You haven't seen him or any of his people at all in the months since the events at Rohde Falls. I know you're not taking bribes, detective. And I would prefer to encourage civility."

"Civility," Palmer repeated. "Coming from the man who put that guy's revered brains all over the wall of his farmhouse."

"You could have stopped me."

"What?"

"You only stood there. You entered that farmhouse, and smelled the death. You heard the sobs of the captive he was most certainly going to kill before I intervened. I spoke to you—imparted my wisdom—and you watched me then impart my justice. And you didn't even raise your weapon."

He was right. That was precisely the way Palmer recalled the series of events. At that moment in time, he knew that the scientist had to die.

He just felt it.

"You talk about justice," Palmer said. "But what about the courts? What about the law's kind of justice?"

"Sometimes justice can only be fabricated by stained hands, detective."

"Stop calling me that," Palmer snapped. "You've been following me around for months, I figure. And you know all the places I go. So you damn well know what my name is."

Mortuary continued to look at him with black, soulless eyes. He either had no response or didn't feel like giving one.

"Something was really wrong with that guy, wasn't it? The way he just kneeled there spouting that gibberish. Like he believed what he was saying. It was a lot like--"

The man cloaked in darkness waited in silence.

"God's Acre."

"You are beginning to understand," Mortuary said.

"What happened to you?" Frank asked. "What have you seen?"

Mortuary took his time in answering. "Things I prefer normal people continue to not see."

"But why?" Palmer raised and lowered a hand with a gesture that encompassed Mortuary's clothing. "Did you just listen to too many radio shows?"

"When you know there's no one left to disappoint—that there will be no one to mourn your passing when you leave the world, one can truly transcend beyond the fear of one's own death. It becomes irrelevant."

Palmer allowed the words to sink in. Mortuary—whoever he was—was clearly an intelligent, well-educated man. He may have hidden his face and knowledge of who he was, but he couldn't hide everything. And the longer they conversed, the more Frank learned about him.

"And you are like me," Mortuary said.

"What?" Frank wasn't expecting that. His tone became one of defiance. "And how exactly is that?"

"I see it in you," Mortuary said. "And I am all too familiar. A darkness that runs so deep that you can never again be anyone's sunshine."

It had taken two years before Frank was willing to have that conversation with his best friend—his brother-in-law at that—he damn sure wasn't about to have it again so soon with a featureless face.

"So let's say you're right. If you've been watching me so long, why are we just now having a discussion about something more than devils?"

"Because I had to make certain I could trust you."

"And do you?" Palmer asked.

"You could have stopped me then. You didn't. If they even believe I exist, then I am likely wanted by the police for questioning. You could attempt to catch me now. But you won't."

"Maybe I don't want to be the man who caught Mortuary."

The gunshots on the street below had ceased a few minutes earlier. Frank knew that Arturo was likely okay, but he hoped the same could be said for Eddie, Lenny, Pete and Henry. Those machine guns...

"We need to put Lucetti out of the German gun business. That has to be who Crocetti is getting them from," Palmer said.

Mortuary nodded. It appeared, at least for now, that he had earned Palmer's trust as well.

"I will handle that."

"Do you think Crocetti killed Maxwell?" Palmer asked.

"It is looking increasingly likely. But you will need to find a way to prove it."

"If Cassano and Donati are working for Crocetti—I've never heard of either of those guys. They might be new enough to flip. But, then again, that's not really the circle I'm familiar with. No matter what, though, pinning the murder on Crocetti isn't going to be easy."

"Then we will need to find something else to pin on Crocetti," Mortuary said.

Palmer nodded in agreement. Maybe they could link the German machine guns he was getting from Lucetti. In a case like that, Lucetti might turn so he could save his own hide.

"Do you think while you're shutting down Lucetti's gun operation, you could see about finding a way to connect them to Crocetti?"

The black hat bobbed up and down.

"I will look into that, as well. Any evidence I find in that regard will be delivered to you."

Palmer turned toward the club. With all that gunfire, Arturo had to have cleared the club by now. Hopefully, the uniforms that showed up would either be on Casadonte's payroll or amiable to the prospect of such.

"The police are going to be on the scene," Palmer said. "I know you'll just disappear like Claude Rains, but I can't be caught in all this shit."

He was going to have to climb down the fire escape and traverse his way through the carnage to get back to the Buick. Palmer hoped none of the mess down there would prevent his speedy departure.

"So," Palmer said. "If there's nothing else for us to discuss?"

"I will be in touch soon," Mortuary said.

By the time Palmer reached the fire escape and turned around, Mortuary was nowhere to be seen.

FOURTEEN

Wednesday, April 14, 1937.

THE GLASS BOUNCED off the wall and, to the surprise of everyone in the room, it didn't break until after it hit the floor.

Benny Cassano and Joey Donati continued to stand by in silence, too afraid to speak until Nico Crocetti had decided that he was going to be finished with his tirade.

The veins in his neck were on display, and Nico's face reddened with a color that Joey would have sworn was on the blue side of purple.

"That son of a bitch," Nico said, knocking a mug of ink pens off his desk. "That selfish, short-sighted son of a bitch! He spites me, I tell you. He spites me from the grave."

The attorney held the paperwork in his hands, but they may as well have been tied. There was nothing he could do to rectify the situation and he felt like he was the least safe person in the room.

The details had been revealed just a few minutes ago. Aside from leaving each of his daughters enough money to remain comfortable for the rest of their days, all of Nico's assets would be sold, with his cash and the sale of those assets all going to the same location.

"Arturo Casadonte!" Nico yelled, still fuming. "Sal Barone, my own brother-in-law—the widower of my sister—he leaves everything to this guy instead of his own flesh and blood? That's faith in your family right there, I tell you. What good's it for? Huh, Joey? What good's it for?"

Joey Two Stacks looked at Benny, hoping the shorter fellow would say something to bail him out. Contrary to his notable demeanor that made him every bit deserving of his nickname, Benny had a talent for calming Mr. Crocetti in situations such as these.

"I—I don't know what to say, Mr. Crocetti."

"You don't say nothing, Joey." Crocetti strode over and shook his finger in Joey's face. "Because chances are no matter what you said, it's not going to be anything I want to hear."

Nico turned to the attorney, glaring. The man took a step back and was currently thinking of making a break for the door.

"And you," Nico said. "You're worth even less. You probably sat there with the executor and August Florian while Casadonte's attorney swindled us out the empire that was supposed to be mine."

"No sir, I—"

Benny drove an elbow into the attorney's side, then shook his head as though he were telling him, He doesn't want an answer right now. Remember what just happened to Joey.

"Oh, thank you for leaving me one of your cars, Mr. Barone," Nico mocked. "It'll be such an honor watching it sit there and rust since I won't be able to afford to put gas in it."

Joey was collecting the pens and stuffing them back into the mug. He sat it within reach on Nico's desk, just in case he wanted to knock it off again.

Crocetti pointed a finger at Benny and Joey.

"Lucetti's new guys bungled the operation last night," he said. "They had automatic weapons, and somehow that detective is still upright and walking the earth today."

"Want us to bring him in?" Benny asked.

"Damn right I do," Nico said.

Then, he turned to the attorney. "And you can get the hell out of here. Your services are no longer needed today."

The attorney was all too happy to be excused. He tossed the paperwork into his briefcase and only closed one of the clasps before he snatched it up and followed a direct path toward the door.

Once the attorney was gone, Crocetti turned to Benny and Joey again.

"On second thought," he said. "Forget about Lucetti for now. You two are going to deal with that detective. He's getting too close to finding out things he doesn't need to be knowing."

"Want us to talk to him and see if he could use some thicker pockets?" Joey asked.

"That ain't going to work," Crocetti said. "From what Lucetti tells me, he was practically arm-in-arm with Casadonte and his boys. What do we got on this detective?"

"Name's Frank Palmer," Benny said. "No family to speak of—at least that we know about. Word is that he had a wife, but she died in thirty-five."

"On Labor Day," Joey added.

Benny continued. "He's been a cop for somewhere around ten years. But the thing is, he ain't on anyone's payroll."

Crocetti furrowed his brow. "If he's not on the take, then what's he doing with Casadonte?"

"That's the thing, Mr. Crocetti," Joey said. "We don't know. Maybe they're old pals or something."

"Any truth to what they're saying about there being a gunman on the roof? That 'Mortuary' from the papers?"

"That's what they say," Benny admitted. "Supposedly he was taking shots at Lucetti's guys, but I have to say that claiming a mystery man from the newspaper was there taking potshots sounds more like somebody trying to keep from looking so bad if you know what I mean."

Nico agreed. Lucetti wasn't one to exaggerate or spin tales, but he had raved about these new guys he was bringing in. And these new guys failed on every level. All they had to do was kill one detective with a revolver.

"Find Frank Palmer," Crocetti said. "Then use him to find that actress—wherever they're hiding her. After you do that, bring her to me. Leave Palmer somewhere on the west side. And if this Mortuary happens to show his face again, kill him too."

"Yes sir," Benny acknowledged.

"Is there anything else, boss?" Joey asked.

Nico unfolded a twenty-dollar bill, extending it toward Benny.

"Sometime while you're out, go by Tammary's and give this to one of the ladies. Tell them to send over whatever that buys."

The two men retrieved their hats from the rack.

Once they were gone, Crocetti picked up the phone and stroked the dial. When someone answered, he spoke to them in a manner of directness.

"It's Nico Crocetti. About that deal I set up between you and Lucetti—after the next shipment you have promised, let's just go ahead and start delivering them to my place. Yes, the factory on Twelfth. Good. I'll be in touch."

Hanging up the telephone, Nico released a sigh. Now he was about to experience the worst part of his day—he had to deliver the bad news. Barone had left them with a shiny car, but that wasn't going to go far in getting the kind of doctors that Myrna needed to improve her condition.

* * * * *

Today was another of her good days. When Nico opened the door, Myrna was up and walking around. Adjusting the flowers in one of the vases, she smiled when he entered.

"Good morning," she said with a sound of pleasantry in her voice.

Nico hugged her from behind and delivered the expected kiss on the cheek.

"You must be feeling better today."

"I am," Myrna said. "But you don't seem to be having one of your better mornings."

"It's that easy to tell, huh?"

Nico sighed and pulled the curtains the rest of the way open.

"Things didn't go as planned this morning," he said. "Or last night. Or this whole rotten week, it's shaping up to look like."

Pulling her attention from the flowers, Myrna joined him at the window.

"Tell me what's wrong," she said.

Nico shook his head and attempted to make the situation lighter than it was. This kind of thing wasn't her burden to bear. She had enough problems as it were without having to throw more on top of the pile.

"Just some things I need to work out. Nothing for you to concern yourself with."

"If it's bothering you, then it affects me plenty," she argued.

He almost spoke, but then hesitated. He just didn't know how the world falling apart was supposed to be put into words.

"I'm a big girl," Myrna said. "I assure you that whatever it is, I can handle it."

"Barone's will," Nico answered. "We didn't get zip. There's a Cadillac, but that's all."

Myrna's eyebrows raised in concern. He was already cursing himself for what this would mean to her.

"What happened?" she asked.

"Arturo Casadonte happened. Apparently, he and Sal went way back. Something to do with this orphanage that

Casadonte stayed in and Arturo saving his life. I don't know the whole story, really."

"How long has he done this to you?" she asked.

Nico took her hand in his, shaking his head.

"Sal was always fair to me. That's why I don't understand how everything—"

"I'm talking about Arturo Casadonte," Myrna said. "Every time you have your fingers on the brass ring, he comes along and snatches it out of your hand. And now, when you only want a slice of bread, he takes the entire loaf, leaving us with the crumbs."

Nico looked into her eyes, seeing something beginning to emerge that he hadn't seen since before she became ill.

Her words also did nothing to prevent his mood from falling back into the state it was earlier in his office.

She turned to him and ran her fingers through his hair. "Nico, you just have to do what needs to be done. If Arturo Casadonte is no longer around, then everything you see out that window—it's all yours. I will have the doctors I need, and then I'll get well—and imagine the life we can have together then."

"It has to be carefully planned," he said. "Someone tried last night and failed, so Casadonte is going to be alert for a while. I need to keep things calm a few weeks, let him relax—enjoy all that money Sal left for him. And when his guard is finally down... The next time I see

Arturo Casadonte, it'll be from the outside of a casket, and he won't have a damn thing to say."

Myrna threw her arms around the back of his neck and initiated a brief dance that the two had not had for some time.

"And then," she said, "I will revel at the sight of his wife and daughters drowning in their own tears."

Nico grinned. He had forgotten how deliciously devious she could be when she was feeling at her best.

Their dance was interrupted by the arrival of Dr. Roth. He regarded the pair curiously for a moment as he sat his bag on the bed and began removing some of the medicines inside.

"Good morning, sir. Ma'am."

"Your timing is incredible, Kent," Myrna said dryly.

"I'm sorry, did I disrupt the conversation?"

"No," Nico said. "It's fine. I'll let you get to your work. I have some things to attend to, myself."

Kissing his wife and bidding her farewell, Nico returned to the hallway. His heart had been heavy when he realized the news he would have to reveal, but he had forgotten the type of woman that Myrna truly was.

Perhaps one day he would cease to underestimate her resolve and the woman herself.

He returned to his office, stepping over the broken glass.

A large number of things were going to break underneath the weight of his path to greatness... Casadonte, that detective, and anyone else who saw fit to get in the way of the construction of his empire's foundation and the wellness of his lovely wife.

FIFTEEN

Thursday, April 15, 1937.

THE HOTEL THAT HAD BEEN set up for Roselyn Farrell was only a few blocks from her apartment. The heads that came together and then made the calls thought it was for the best to almost hide her in plain sight, and the hotel had most of the amenities she was accustomed to living with: room service, a spacious bath, and a bar completely stocked with brandy. The twenty-four-hour guard posted outside her door was complimentary.

Palmer showed his badge to the guard and knocked on the door. To his knowledge, no one had been looking for Roselyn since her temporary living arrangements were made and with him closing in on the possibility of being able to put Maxwell's murder on Nico Crocetti, it was only a matter of time before she would be able to go home.

But with eyes on him now, he needed to be able to get to his meeting with Arturo Casadonte without being seen. And to pull that off, he would need some assistance.

The door swung open, and Frank was met with a warm smile from the glamorous blonde, welcoming him inside.

Palmer removed his hat politely.

"Good afternoon, Ms. Farrell—"

"Rose," she said.

"That's right. I just wanted to come by and see how you were doing. I'm sorry I haven't had time before now."

As he would have expected, Rose was making her way to the bar. Pouring a drink, she looked up to him with another smile.

"That's understandable," she said, raising her glass. "Detective Callaghan graced me with his company yesterday. I think he's a fan."

Palmer hung his hat on the rack nearby. Callaghan did say that he had seen the picture with his wife. Frank recalled that he liked it.

"It's good to see you again, though," Rose said. "At least, for once, this time, it is under more pleasant circumstances."

His expression grew cold. Frank was going to have to tell her more than he wanted about the events that had taken place over the course of the past few days. He thought that she was likely out of danger, but he couldn't be entirely sure of that. Not with everything that was going on with the major players.

"I don't know any of our interactions will ever be without complication, I'm afraid."

Rose tilted her head, wondering what he meant by that.

Frank sighed and decided things would go more quickly if he refrained from any bush-beating.

"I think we know who killed Maxwell. You were right—it looks like the mob was involved and all signs are pointing to Nicodemus Crocetti as the shot caller. Now I just have to prove it. But that's looking up, too, because that's who those two men from the other night are working for."

Swirling the glass, Rose seemed to be relieved. No arrest had been made, but Palmer felt that having some answers was a growing comfort to her.

"So, you found them, then?" Rose asked.

Frank shook his head. "No, not yet. But one of my contacts identified them. We have an APB on them now, so it's only a matter of time before they stick their necks out."

She was dressed to the hilt. Temporarily residing in an unfamiliar place that didn't feel like home had ensured that Rose wouldn't be answering the door again unprepared. This time, it was a black dress. The only thing she was missing was her heels and Frank only noticed this due to the sound her stockinged feet made as they padded across the floor.

"What about...the third man?" There was trepidation in her voice.

Palmer threw up his hands. "The papers do a good job of making it sound like fictional accounts, so most people don't even believe he's real. No one is even looking for him. It makes it hard to put that kind of thing in the report, so, for now, we're just leaving that part out—saying you slugged one of them and managed to get out the door."

"But you believe me, right? That he was there?"

"Yes, I believe you," Frank said.

Rose emptied the glass and sat it on an end table.

"That's a relief," she said. "After I had collected myself that night, I had to question that it had even happened. I've read the stories in *The Amendment*, but even after seeing it, I just didn't know."

"He may have saved your life. I don't know exactly what those two men wanted with you the other night," Frank said," but I think my connection with you is the reason that someone is out to get me now, too."

"Out to get you? How?" Rose asked.

"I haven't figured it out yet. But until I do, we're going to have to insist that you stay here just a little longer. A precaution for your own protection. I'm not sure how deep Maxwell was in it, but there's someone out there who's trying to make sure I don't get any closer to finding out."

"What do you mean?" Rose asked.

"There was an...incident last night. Some shots were fired."

She held her hand to her open mouth. "Someone tried to kill you?"

Her concern was genuine. Although the physical reaction was a little dramatic, that probably came with the training that came from being an actress. Frank had heard that even stage performers had a habit of doing things in ordinary life as they'd been taught to do when performing. Sometimes they forgot that they weren't on stage—or in her case—in front of the camera.

What he didn't expect, though, was for the woman to draw as close as she did. Rose placed her hands on the lapels of his coat.

"Yes, but I'm all right," he said, tempted to take a step back.

It was only with the rare exception that Palmer was comfortable with someone standing that close to him.

"I'm glad," she said. "I didn't mean to draw you into all this. Especially not having you shot at."

Palmer shrugged, taking her wrists gently so that he could remove her hands from his coat.

"It's okay," he said. "Sometimes it just goes with the territory—part of the job."

"And do you ever have time for anything that isn't part of the job?" Rose asked.

Frank then realized that he still hadn't let her hands go. Nor had he pulled them from his coat.

Before he could answer, she stood on the ends of her toes, pressing her lips to his.

Frank hesitated, closing his eyes. It had been so long since he had felt a woman's touch—the tenderness of the way her soft mouth felt against his...

Her arms wrapped around his neck and he put his hands around her waist, allowing the kiss to happen while he was lost in the moment.

But when his senses overcame the euphoria of a sensation that almost felt new again, he finally tore her arms away from him, drawing back.

Rose looked up at him, confusion evident on her striking features.

"I'm sorry," Frank said. "God knows I am, Rose. But I can't do this."

She withdrew as though she had been struck.

"I—I'm so embarrassed," she said. "When I didn't see a ring on your hand when you came to my apartment, I assumed you weren't married."

Palmer gripped his forehead in his hand. "I'm not. I was. I just...damn it, I should go."

Her cheeks were red, and her first instinct was to return to the bar and fill that glass as far as it would go. She practically stomped her way there.

Frank snatched his hat from the rack. She had nothing to be ashamed of. It was a tired old saying, but the fact of the matter was that it was indeed him—not her—that was the problem. It was something that he missed greatly, but having that type of moment with someone else would have diluted the way he remembered things. Pursuing it would feel like a betrayal.

"Look, I'm sorry," he said. "You're one of the most beautiful woman I've ever seen—I truly mean that. You're smart, funny and talented. And no, I haven't seen it, but I'm sure anyone who saw your picture and didn't like it is just a sap who doesn't know what he's talking about."

The softness of her mouth was gone as she paraphrased his words.

"But you're not, you were, and you should go."

"Yeah." Securing his hat, Palmer crowned himself king of fools.

This was a complication he couldn't afford, considering the primary reason he had come by to check on her in the first place.

"I'm sorry if I embarrassed you," Palmer said. "But I need to ask a favor."

Rose silently glared from the other side of the room.

"I'm meeting with one of my contacts tonight to get further insight into the case, but I think I'm being followed. Not here, though—I checked," Frank clarified. "But my car is pretty recognizable, and I need to be able to have this thing undetected."

She knew what he was asking. The soft falls of her feet on the floor was the only sound in the suite of uncomfortable and resounding silence for a moment. Rose disappeared into the bedroom, pulling the hotel key from the ring and tossing the rest to him.

"Thanks," he said, shoving the keys into his pocket. "And don't worry, I'll take good care of it. Things could run late tonight, so I'll have it back to you in the morning."

She escorted him to the door, closing it behind him without uttering another word.

* * * * *

The parking lot of the small arena was already packed with cars. The steering in Rose's 1935 Ford Coupe was a little different from the smooth handling of the Buick, but Frank had been able to manage once he had gotten used to the suspension pulling the car slightly to the left.

He had replayed the events a few times in his mind, keeping his eyes on the mirrors. He knew the adage about a woman scorned, but with focus on ensuring that he hadn't been tailed from the hotel, Palmer had only given passing concern to the thoughts of what fury may arise from a woman rejected.

After circling the area several times and watching for headlights that never resigned, he had been suitably convinced that he wasn't shadowed.

Frank had found a parking spot in the largest medley of vehicles—perhaps he was being overly cautious, but losing the Ford in the shuffle would help to alleviate any concerns of being spotted—no matter who the onlooker might have been.

Considering the amount of cars at the auditorium, he imagined he was late. When Palmer saw Arturo Casadonte standing out front smoking a cigarette, he was certain of it.

"Sorry," Frank said. "I got held up with some things with the Maxwell case."

Arturo shrugged. "You haven't missed much. There was a pretty good team bout that started things off, and there's a girls' match going on now, so I figured I'd come out and wait for you."

"Girls?" Frank asked.

"Yeah, that's been going on awhile. I don't think there was one on the card last time we came." Casadonte extinguished his cigarette in the gravel of the tall receptacle beside him. "They even have a Women's World Champion and everything."

When they were heading into the building, Arturo showed the doorman two ticket stubs, throwing his head in Palmer's direction as they passed.

"He's with me."

Frank immediately heard the sound of the crowd booing whatever was going on, though he couldn't see it from the lobby area.

"Crowd sounds hot," Frank observed.

"Yeah, and we're in the front row, so it should make for an interesting night."

The pair entered the main part of the arena just in time to see a dark-haired woman in a black one-piece bathing suit leap into the air and come crashing down across the upper chest of her opponent with all her body weight, crushing the girl beneath her. The crowd exploded into cheers as the referee glided into position on the mat to make the three count. The cheering continued as the woman was awarded the championship belt, securing it around her waist.

"See," Arturo gestured to the ring as he led Frank to their seats, "I told you."

With the match over, a refreshment girl approached just as they had taken their seats. She was dressed in an elaborate red and black costume with a short skirt that came just above the knees and stockings, which not only distinguished her from any of the other women in the building but also made it verifiable that she wasn't a lady wrestler.

"Can I get you gentlemen anything?" She smiled.

Casadonte waved her off with a hand, shaking his head.

"How about you, sir?" She asked Palmer.

Frank considered for a moment and then made a decision. "You got a pack of Chesterfield Kings in that box?"

She smiled, reaching into the box strapped around the back of her neck so that it was held out before her alluring figure.

"You can get two packs for twenty-five cents."

Frank reached into his pocket, producing a quarter. "Let's do that."

The exchange was made, and the woman moved on to the next group in the front row.

Frank opened the pack and offered one to Arturo.

"I'm going to assume that since you don't look heartbroken, that everything went okay after I left last night."

Arturo nodded, lighting his cigarette. "Eddie said those guys scrambled pretty fast right after you disappeared. But Pete Aronstein is kind of steamed with you."

"What? Why is that?"

"Well, for starters, he almost died." It wouldn't have been a laughing matter had the turn taken a different course. "Says the machinegun you slid over to them didn't have any bullets in it."

"Shit," Palmer said. "It was dark. I thought that was the other one."

Arturo chuckled. "He just picked up and tried to start firing away."

The ring announcer made his presence known, and Frank had to talk over his introductions for the next match on the card.

"How's business going?"

"Not too well at the moment," Casadonte said. "Things were looking up until Finely Done Recession had to do some more meddling and 'fix' the recovery until it was broken."

"Why is that?" Frank asked.

"Excise taxes, for starters." He nodded to the cigarette girl down the line. "You just paid twenty-five cents for two packs of cigarettes. They're taxing most of the things normal people buy, so the middle and lower class is stuck paying for this operation. Everything from cigarettes to playing cards to tires—they even tax the tires on wheelchairs, for crying out loud."

"On wheelchairs?" Frank had feigned disbelief, although he was beginning to wish he hadn't opened the floodgates.

"Just another Democrat with big promises he can never deliver on. I was going to expand the textile factory and open another in the location I have on Fourteenth Street, but now that falls under his anti-chain whatever you call it—so even if I wanted to pay the increased taxes on Social Security, I can't hire those five hundred people and put them to work. I'm getting pretty tired of being told what to do in my own business by some bureaucratic attorney who's never held anything but his momma's dress, an elected position that he got by spinning tales and his Johnson in his hand so he can wave it around at everybody. And to make matters worse, you got these union assholes going on strike during a time when everybody else who has a job is just happy to have one."

"You could start taking those unions over—I heard that's what Lucetti and some of the others were doing with their businesses. Turn the tables, make them work for you and at least give the impression you're on their side."

"And get in bed with the federal government?" Casadonte looked like he had just taken a bite of a lemon. "I may do some questionable things from time to time in my line of work, but I don't swim in that shit."

"Well, maybe one day they'll judge these government programs on their actual results, not their good intentions," Frank said.

The crowd around them was cheering the largest man Frank had ever seen. The top ring rope fell somewhere between his waist and his lower chest. He must have weighed well over three hundred pounds.

When the crowd calmed down a little, Frank and Arturo heard a voice behind them.

"Real big mouth. Some kind of real man you are. Sitting there in the front row with your thirty-dollar suit and complaining about the man who's trying to fix things."

Casadonte turned around to see that the man was looking directly at him. He was about their age, slender and a little rough around the edges while not bothering to go home and change clothes after he had gotten off the construction site.

Arturo straightened the lapels of his jacket. "Actually, the suit was thirty-two dollars."

Frank winced. There was likely about to be a fight outside the ring as well as one inside—Arturo wasn't going to feel the need to get paid for it, either. He trained with Eddie Pierce two hours every day, so if this guy behind them wanted a fight, he wasn't going to have a ghost of a chance. Especially since he was the skinniest construction worker Palmer had ever seen.

The man behind them rose to his feet, flicking the ash from his cigar.

"When I can get the work, I'll bust my hump ten hours a day just so I can put food on the table for my wife and little ones. I can barely get by and then I got to watch people like you running around living the high life and sitting in the front row."

Arturo continued to look up at him, turned around in his seat as the man pointed his cigar at him like it was his finger.

"And yet you spent the quarter and nickel getting in here—God only knows how much that big cigar set you back."

Palmer found it considerably fortunate for the man that Casadonte wasn't taking his insults seriously just yet. Otherwise, that family was going to have a lot more problems when the father and husband was discovered face-down in an alley somewhere.

The man ignored the truth in Arturo's statement, as people who are wrong and are too stupid to know it are wanton to do.

"And another thing..." the construction worker said. "That's the office of the President you're disrespecting. No matter what he does, you should support his decision when he's just trying to help everyone. My old man came back wounded from the war—bled for this country so people like you could strut around in your thirty-two dollar suits. What did yours do from his palatial estate— shed a tear or two for the dead?"

Frank saw that Arturo's knuckles were turning white from the grip he had on the arm of his chair. He was now going to have to intervene and save this guy's life before things got out of hand.

"You need to shut your mouth and sit back down," Palmer said. "Before I sit you down."

The man gestured at Frank with his cigar. "Tough guy, huh? Are you talking to me?"

"Well, evidently," Palmer said. "Because it's too late for me to catch whoever taught you your god damn manners."

When he began to step toward them, Palmer pulled his coat aside and revealed the badge attached to his belt.

"In fact," Palmer said, "I think you should find yourself another seat, or you'll get a police escort and a foot in the ass to send you out the front door."

The people directly behind them watched to see what the construction worker would do. After a few seconds of weighing his options, he chose the better part of valor and turned away, heading toward the arena stairs.

Casadonte turned back to Palmer. "Good work, detective. I was about to drag that guy out back and let him meet the real me."

"Yeah," Frank said. "I'd like to get out of here tonight without one of us having something incriminating in the trunk."

The big man in the ring delivered an overhand right that sent his opponent careening flat on his back on the canvas. He then pinned the man with little effort.

When the crowd was on their feet, Arturo nodded as if he had just remembered something.

"And getting rid of evidence reminds me—the executor got the will all squared away. Your Uncle Sal left about three-thousand dollars that he wanted me to give to you."

Palmer was surprised. "Jesus, Arthur, how am I supposed to—"

"I'll have August write you a check. He already gave you a car for saving his ass the second time he ever got shot at—as he calls it—so it won't be coming directly from me."

The ring announcer informed the audience that the time for the main event was at hand. While Arturo leaned forward to get a glimpse of the champ when he made his appearance, Frank was sitting back and contemplating the ramifications of suddenly having three-thousand dollars at his disposal.

Realizing that the opponent was going to come out first, Casadonte leaned back toward Palmer.

"After last night—I can't let that go—we're going to move on Crocetti and put an end to this once and for all."

"When?" Frank asked.

"It's going down as soon as I get out of here tonight. We've got a line on his current whereabouts—"

"No," Frank said.

Palmer saw the business end of Arturo Casadonte rising to the surface. That wasn't a word the mob boss had often heard in his adult life.

"What do you mean no?"

Palmer navigated carefully. He wanted to tell Arturo that the attempted hit wasn't actually on him, but the fact remained that it still happened at his club, which made it his business.

"I've got something in the pipeline. I think I can connect him to Lucetti. And Lucetti to those guns they're getting from the Heinies. If I can do that, then we can take him out of the game legally. He'll be gone for a long time. And then, whatever happens to him in prison—well..."

"And then what happens when I'm the only game in town? When I'm King Arthur?"

Frank couldn't help but chuckle—he sincerely hoped that wouldn't be what they called him.

"Nothing," Frank said. "Because if they ever make me choose between you and them, I'll leave the badge laying on the desk."

Arturo smirked. "And then you could always come work for me. The boys like you—well, except for maybe Aronstein at the moment, but he'll get over it—but I can assure you the money would be better than whatever pension you expect you'll be getting."

Frank shook his head. "I always figured that when I was done there, I'd go into business for myself—be a private investigator."

"In that case," Arturo said, "I bet three-thousand dollars is making you do a lot more figuring. Aw, now look at this bum here—he's not championship material—Detton is going to kill him."

The opponent moved down the aisle to a chorus of boos. He could have been six feet tall, tops. To Frank, he looked like they had just plucked someone out of the crowd and asked him if he wanted to get in the ring with the champ.

"So... Are we in agreement? You'll let me see what I can do about Crocetti? And if I can't get him on the guns, then you can handle it your way?"

"What about Maxwell? You can't get him on that?"

Frank sighed. "We're not getting anywhere with that. Since it wasn't you, that makes it Crocetti by process of elimination, but it's not about what I know, it's about what I can prove—which, so far, isn't a damn thing."

"Sure, I can wait," Casadonte nodded. "But I'm not going to wait long. If your way doesn't produce results soon, I'm going to do it the Salvadore Barone way."

They leaped to their feet with the rest of the crowd when the World Heavyweight Champion could be seen coming down the aisle.

Arturo donned a mischievous grin, turning to Frank. "Come on, do it. What he said that time the Bianco Family tried to put people in with us, to take him out, back in thirty-three."

Palmer sighed. He was a little rusty, but he did his best to get into character as Salvadore Barone. "When you and your people—when you get out there in those woods, Frankie, you know what you a'gonna find?"

Both men answered the nostalgic question at the same time.

"Seven souls of seven sons a'bitches who kept digging holes when they should have been building mountains."

SIXTEEN

HE HAD CONSIDERED parking near the old white house, just to mull over the situation with Nico Crocetti and all the problems that came with it, but Palmer took a right turn at the last minute, deciding that the drive home would be sufficient.

The hour was already late.

So, Morgan Maxwell owed Crocetti well over a thousand dollars. The mob boss probably sent one—maybe two—of his strong arms to collect and when that failed, they levied on Maxwell permanently.

It could have even been one or both of the two men who had gone to Roselyn Farrell's apartment and slapped her around until Mortuary showed up.

The ledger books Maxwell kept were an indicator, but with the method in which they were scribed, those were still not enough to indict Crocetti on murder charges—especially with one of the three missing.

Palmer only wondered what incriminating evidence could have been in the one from nineteen thirty-six.

He pulled the black Ford into his driveway, making sure the doors were locked before he departed the vehicle.

Something had made him a person of interest to Crocetti, but he couldn't wrap his mind around what that was just yet. It had to be something related to Rose Farrell. Maybe she knew more than she was letting on.

Palmer would discuss that with her when he returned her car in the morning.

Fishing the keys out of his pocket, he remembered that he hadn't locked the front door—in fact, he didn't really recall the last time he had been home. And a shower was a much-needed event.

Palmer tossed the keys on the coffee table in the den and made his way through the dimly lit little dining room that was adjoined to the kitchen.

He knew it would keep him up the rest of the night, but Palmer desired coffee even more than the shower, so he filled the pot with water and delivered it to the stove.

While he was waiting for the water to boil, he thought some reading would help to take his mind out of reality for a little while, but when he flipped the light switch in the living room, Palmer discovered that he wasn't alone.

He cursed himself for not noticing that one of the chairs was missing from the dining room.

Presently, it was in his living room and filled by an occupant. It was Donnie, that kid from two houses down. Palmer didn't know him that well, but in his experience, the kid had been somewhat annoying. Frank was pretty sure it was Donnie and his friends who were responsible for tearing up his grass that time.

Donnie looked at Palmer with wide eyes, though he didn't speak or move a muscle.

Behind the kid stood a short, rather wide man dressed in business attire. His nose was red and swollen, and the area beneath his eyes was a shade somewhere between purple and black. The .45 he held was an indication of his seriousness regarding the current situation.

"Look," Palmer said, "I don't know what he did this time, but you've got the wrong house."

He was moving his hand toward his coat when the sound of a hammer being drawn stopped him in his tracks.

A voice from behind him was deep, barely above a whisper. "Don't move."

Frank knew the gun was aimed at the back of his head.

The short man standing behind Donnie had his hat pulled low on his brow. He stared at Palmer for a moment, sizing him up.

"Do you know who I am?" The man asked.

Palmer shrugged. "No, I sure don't. So that tells me you must not be one of the worth-a-shits."

He knew good and well that it was Benny Cassano. That was most likely Joey Donati behind him.

Benny made a face as if to say wise ass! And nodded his head a few times.

"I ain't one for wasting a bunch of time with talking, so here's what's going to happen... Take that piece out of the shoulder holster and toss it on the floor. And I think you know how this works. You make any kind of threatening move and me and the kid are going to take a shower in your brains. Then I'm going to put one in this little shit sitting right here."

Benny leveled his pistol at the back of Donnie's head.

"And this just happens to be my favorite suit," Benny said. "So it's up to you, cowboy."

Palmer glanced over to the bookshelf. They had apparently been reading his old books and magazines to pass the time while waiting for him to show up.

He slowly reached into his coat and pulled Maurice from security, discarding the revolver as instructed.

"Now, here's what we do next," Benny said. "You'll take us to where your people are hiding that washed up actress. Our employer wants to have some words with her in person."

"What does Crocetti want with her?" Palmer asked.

"Hey, look," Joey snickered, "He's a detective after all."

"I don't know. That's between him and her. But you don't need to worry about that right now."

"Okay," Palmer said. "But you're going to have to let the kid go, first."

"Not happening. The kid is going with us. He's our little insurance policy to make sure you come back out with her and don't try to skip out on us."

Frank was confident now that Rose had to know more than she pretended to—those acting chops had paid off. Was she somehow hiding cash for Maxwell? That had to be it. Just as he had told Callaghan, a lot of the time it was over money.

They were supposedly estranged, but every two weeks Maxwell would show up to her apartment with flowers.

What if they weren't really split? It could have been a cleverly-devised cover for Maxwell to make bi-weekly cash deliveries to her under the guise of trying to woo his girl back into his arms.

And Palmer would bet his Buick that the details of these arrangements were in the missing book.

Maxwell and Rose had to have been ripping off Crocetti.

She was an actress—Maxwell was a radio personality, so he had the natural gift of gab. His fast talking could get him another so-called loan, while her acting talents would throw everyone off the trail by giving the impression that she was finished with him.

But when Maxwell had taken Crocetti for a comfortably substantial sum, where would they have gone to escape his vengeance once he put the pieces together?

Paris.

Palmer might have a chance now. These two goons standing in his living room were likely the direct tie to getting Crocetti on murder, as well as the possibility of the European guns.

Benny leveled his pistol at Palmer and waved the weapon in the direction of the front door.

"So let's get moving," Benny said. "We ain't got all night."

Frank slowly turned in the direction of the door, keeping his hands aloft. Joey took a step back, his .45 remaining on the detective.

"Move it, kid," Palmer heard Benny say to Donnie.

The screeching of the coffee pot brought to a boil startled everyone in the house.

Palmer sprang into action, wrapping his arm over Joey's, he grabbed the man's wrist and twisted the arm back toward his head, just like he'd seen Dean Detton do earlier in the night. Frank believed it was called a 'top wrist lock.'

The pressure caused Joey to drop the gun, and Palmer threw him onto the floor with all his strength.

Frank whirled around just in time to see Donnie push Benny's arm so that the bullet aimed for Palmer hit the wall instead. Benny shoved Donnie with his other arm, sending the kid skidding across the floor and set up to fire again.

But Palmer was already on top of him. The right cross he delivered knocked Benny's hat from his head and Frank took the pistol from his hand as Benny stumbled backward.

Joey tackled Palmer's legs from behind, causing his knees to buckle. The two men rolled on the floor jockeying for control as Benny entered the fray once more.

Frank was able to block most of the kick to the ribs with his elbow and bicep, but the momentary lack of protection allowed Joey the opening to rattle Palmer's jaw.

Struggling to his feet, Joey had a firm grasp on his jacket and Benny took another swing. Palmer bobbed his head to the side, narrowly avoiding the blow and shoved Joey away from him.

Benny launched himself toward Frank like a raging bull, and the two men flew five feet through the air before landing hard on the floor. Benny's hands were all over Palmer's face, trying his best to dig his short, meaty fingers into Frank's eyes.

Palmer took the low road in a situation that was not the time for fairness, driving his knee upward between

Benny's legs. The hired killer's body instantly went limp, and Frank pushed off the floor with his foot, rolling Benny's weight off him.

Joey was suddenly there, brandishing a closed umbrella. He took a stab at Palmer with the metal tip. Frank easily batted the umbrella aside and scanned the floor for a gun.

The second time Joey swung the umbrella, it caught Frank on the side of the neck. His coat collar blocked most of the impact, but it still stung like being hit with a strip of leather.

He snatched the umbrella from Joey's hands and grabbed each end, thrusting it long-ways into Joey's face. When Joey stepped back, Palmer cast the worthless makeshift weapon aside.

One of the pistols belonging to the assailants was about three feet away, but before Palmer could get to it, Benny was on his feet and hobbling toward him again.

The shorter man threw up his arm to block the punch Frank had intended for him and Benny dove at him again. When the two went down this time, the back of Palmer's head bounced off the hardwood floor.

Benny looked over and saw that Joey had his lighter in hand, putting flame to the living room curtains.

"Let's go!" Joey called out.

Wincing, Benny returned to a standing position and limped in the direction of the front door. There was no way he was going to be able to fight any longer in his current condition.

Leaving their weapons behind, the two men made their exit as the curtains burst into flames like paper alight.

Smoke began to fill the room.

Donnie emerged from behind the sofa, rushing over to Palmer. Grabbing his shoulder, Donnie shook him a few times.

"Mr. Palmer! You've got to get up. The house is on fire."

Frank was stirring, trying to return to his senses. He touched the back of his head and scanned his hand for blood. There was nothing present, but he was sure there would be such, in the form of a knot, on the back of his head within the hour.

He blinked a few times and looked up to Donnie.

"What?" Palmer asked.

"The skinny guy lit the drapes," Donnie said.

Frank saw the curtains ablaze. The flames were stretching upward like orange tendrils licking at the ceiling by that point and parts of the wall on either side were engulfed.

"Get out of here, kid. I'll be out in a minute."

Panic was not a sensation Frank Palmer regarded as being familiar, but it was the one he was feeling now. He rolled over and removed himself from the floor like a track athlete launching from the starting line.

Rushing into the bedroom, Palmer tore open the drawer of the nightstand, causing his wedding ring to bounce against the wood paneling in the front of the drawer. He slipped the gold band over his finger and snatched a framed photo from within—the only other item in the nightstand.

It was a photograph of Cesca, taken in nineteen thirty-two. She was twenty-five years old at the time, and although there were newer ones developed in the three years that followed, this particular grainy still had always been his favorite.

Frank took a moment to open the front of the frame stand, looking at the colorless beauty within. He had admired the photo most nights, returning it to the drawer before turning in for bed.

The color had been fading from his memories of her for the past two years.

Snapping the front closed, he hurried to the closet. Smoke billowed into the room, clutching tightly to the ceiling, desperate to find an escape. If the front rooms were fully enveloped by the time he was finished here, Frank would have to leave through the back door.

Nearly pulling the closet door from the hinges, Frank rummaged through the stack of boxes in the back corner, unsure now which of those relics from a life packed away contained the brightest treasures.

Finding the box with the rest of their photos, packed securely for their protection with some of her scarves, Frank withdrew it from the corner.

He walked a brisk pace back to the living room, where he was convinced he would see it in flames.

Instead, Palmer saw Donnie standing near the window with a bucket in his hand. What remained of the curtains dripped wet soot onto the already soaked floor, turning it black.

"You're lucky I caught it before it got too out of control," Donnie said. "It really wasn't that bad."

Donnie had thoroughly doused the flames.

Frank sighed, sitting the box on the coffee table.

"Go home," Frank said. "Wait for me on the front porch. It's probably best if I explain this to your parents."

Before the kid left, Palmer unrolled a five-dollar bill from his pocket and handed it to him.

"Good work, kid."

If he had been involved in the mutilation of Palmer's lawn, it would be forgiven and forgotten now.

Donnie took the money, looking at it twice to make sure that's how much it was. He offered his gratitude and crumpled the five into his pants pocket on his way out the door.

Palmer took a long look around the living room. He had nearly lost it all. As the agitation began to subside within him, there was only one emotion that could fill the void.

He plugged the telephone into the wall and picked up the receiver. Dialing the number with purpose, he was patched through to the proper destination.

The wolves had come to his den.

They had threatened a kid and tried to kill him by setting fire to his home.

And worse than all that, they had almost destroyed what little there was left of the thing he loved the most.

When the unfamiliar voice answered the call, Frank said, "Yeah, let me speak to him."

The person on the other end asked who was calling. He spoke the name of the same pseudonym that he always used in the rare instances he had to make a call such as this.

"Tell him it's Aston Glass."

SEVENTEEN

During the lightless hours that live a fleeting existence before dawn, within that obscurity bares the teeth of the things that men fear.

The old factory lay on the waterfront in the industrial area of the city. Shut down during the dawn of the Depression, the lone black-clad figure on the roof was only concerned with one fact regarding the dilapidated structure.

It was abandoned, but not empty.

The factory was well-staffed for a place that was supposedly shut down but gaining entry posed no effort to the figure cloaked in nightfall.

The pistols would draw too much attention, so the secondary armament would make a more convenient option.

The Mark I trench knife had remained unused and sheathed in the right boot for as long as he could remember. He wrapped his fingers into the knuckle bows and withdrew nearly seven inches of double-edged steel. The black oxide finished blade was made for both thrusting and slashing strokes and fittingly bore great resemblance to an assassin's dagger. The bow of each cast bronze knuckle of the handle possessed an individual spike that also made the weapon deadly in hand-to-hand combat.

The first man patrolling the inside of the perimeter never had time to realize what had happened to him. Perhaps it was best for him that way.

The only sound made in the one-sided exchange was the whispered gurgling of a throat pierced as easily and casually as the air itself. His body was caught and lowered to the floor with an ironic gentleness before being dragged to a place where it would not be discovered within the next few hours.

Moving as a specter through the halls of the decrepit edifice, there was a good reason the newspapers had christened him with the name that they had.

The silence may as well have been filled with the brass symphony of trumpets; the blood that pounded in his ears may as well have been artillery, and working within the confines of the tight corridors made the man in black feel truly alive.

Tonight, however, the mission was to keep the enemy casualties limited. Only those whose deaths were necessary would find solace unprepared.

When he came upon the second of the after dark sentinels, the man in black allowed the guard to see him before being punched in the face with the spikes on the knife's handle, making it impossible to discern which part of the injuries were from puncture wounds and which were delivered by the blunt force of a man consumed with laying devils to rest.

The third guard found a fortune he would never know existed, as his location was not in a particular environment that put him between the intruder and his destination.

Further along the twisting and intersecting hallways, a voice could be heard.

"It's happening now? Okay, I'll let the boss know. Yes, we're on our way!"

The origin of the voice was rushing out of one of the side rooms when he was caught in the center of the chest by the twisting of a knife.

Moving deeper into the bowels of the building, the figure found satisfaction when he discovered that one of the large warehouse areas was inhabited by the verminous form of Gyp Lucetti.

The vertically challenged Italian man drew a finger across his whisker-like moustache as he stood with several of his enforcers, all gazing upon the shroud as if they had seen a ghost.

Lucetti began yelling at his men, coercing them with furious hand gestures in an attempt to steal their attention from the figure that had yet to flinch.

None of the men drew their weapons; they simply threw the last of the crates carrying the MP18s onto the back of a truck and swarmed into their vehicles.

The figure methodically returned the knife to his boot and drew his pistols to deliver a few parting shots as they made their escape.

He didn't make any true attempt to stop them, and the parting shots were merely part of the facade.

With the guns in his possession, Lucetti would lead him to the whereabouts of Nico Crocetti.

And he would make sure Palmer was waiting.

The detective was almost ready.

EIGHTEEN

THE BACK WINDOW exploded as Joey Donati leaped into the car and gripped the steering wheel, while repeatedly yelling, "It's a hit!"

Nicodemus Crocetti was lying in the back seat, covered in blood, yelling for him to go. Benny Cassano barely made it into the car, slamming the door before Joey stomped the pedal and squealed the tires.

Caught completely off-guard, it had been a veritable slaughter. Nico was in the process of getting word from Benny and Joey when the bullets started flying.

The two had returned, informing him of their failure to apprehend Frank Palmer and use him to find Rose Farrell. Benny still wasn't walking straight, had a broken nose almost twice the width of normal, and now Joey was developing two black eyes to match Benny's, caused from a stiff umbrella shot across the face.

They had been at the warehouse where Nico typically did business with people who couldn't be seen at his office—the sordid type that the police were either on the lookout for or would be if they had ever been spotted with Crocetti.

Mickey Clean was already there, wearing his hat that always reminded everyone of a newspaper boy. In a manner of height, Mickey fell somewhere between Benny Cassano and Joey Donati, though he was older than the both of them.

Mickey was a former bag man for Salvadore Barone, but an incident in which Mickey accidentally killed one of the payoffs left Barone no choice but to cut him loose. Sal didn't like what he called 'loose cannons' and although Mickey had exhibited no such behavior in the past, the fallout with the rest of Barone's protection racket was enough that an example had to be made.

Having built up a reputation, Mickey had found it relatively easy to fall in with Crocetti once the availability of his services was made known.

When lead started cutting flesh, everyone's first instinct was to keep Nico from getting hit. They then tried their best to return fire while making a getaway.

Joey took a hard turn, almost causing Benny to drop his pistol on the floor. Although he had left his other one at Frank Palmer's house, he had a good backup. He still needed to replace his hat, though.

"You hit?" Benny asked Joey.

Joey responded in the negative and Benny leaned out the window to squeeze off a few shots at the five men on foot who were still shooting at them from behind.

"That was Eddie Pierce," Joey said. "I recognize that square-head anywhere."

"No shit," Crocetti called from the back seat. "Of course they were sent by Casadonte—who else would it be?"

Benny returned to his seat. "They ain't following us anymore."

Crocetti sat up. He looked as if someone had thrown a bucket of red paint directly into his face and chest.

Benny pulled a handkerchief from his pocket and waved it toward the back seat. Nico was able to get most of the blood out of his eyes but then looked like he had a red face with a raccoon mask the color of his skin.

Nico threw the handkerchief back into the front seat.

"Where the hell was Lucetti?"

"I don't know, Mr. Crocetti," Benny said. "I don't know."

"You said you called him."

"I did," Benny defended. "I talked to his man Lowell. He said they were on the way. Might even be there getting killed right this minute."

Nico leaned back in the seat, quietly dusting glass fragments from his shoulder.

"Where to?" Joey asked.

"My office."

"What?" Benny protested, turning around. "They might be going there next—that's precisely the place they'd expect to find us."

Nico's cold eyes locked with Benny's. For a moment he didn't say anything—just sat behind him staring. He was making his best effort to calm down before he pulled his pistol and shot Benny right there on the spot.

"That's why we're going to get my wife," Nico said. "Benny. We'll also switch cars while we're there. This shot up hunk won't make for keeping us unnoticed."

The car pulled up to Crocetti's office, and they were all quite thankful that the sun hadn't risen yet. The area out front was silent and devoid of bystanders.

"Park the car, Joey," Crocetti said. "Benny, come with me."

Benny gave Joey a look that warned him to be on his guard before joining their employer on the front steps of the building. He watched Joey drive around the corner before turning to accompany Nico inside.

"You did the right thing tonight, Benny."

"Thanks, Mr. Crocetti. We did the best we could out there, but hell broke loose so fast..."

"No need for excuses or apologies. I'm still alive, and you're still going to keep getting paid."

Benny nodded, and the two men entered the building, with Benny holding the door and taking a second to scan the block before ducking inside.

"What are we going to do now about Casadonte?" Benny asked.

"I want you to make some calls—get everyone together. Find out what happened to Lucetti—see where he is. Then, get in touch with the Gambinos—all of them. I'm going to get Myrna ready to go. After that, we'll take my new car to the factory on Twelfth and figure out where to go from there."

Nico never suspected that the moment would arrive so quickly that he was thankful for the Cadillac left to him by his departed brother-in-law.

"Looks like no one came here after the shootout at the factory," Benny said as they maneuvered the hallways and stepped onto the elevator.

The elevator man regarded the crimson-covered Nico with a curious bewilderment, standing there with his hand on the lever as if he had suddenly forgotten how to do his job.

"Tenth floor," Benny said coldly.

The man finally remembered and threw the lever. Whatever trouble these men had seen wasn't something he wanted to be around for when it followed.

Nico and Benny exited the elevator and went directly to Myrna's room. Nico turned the handle without bothering to knock.

With the curtains closed, Benny couldn't see a thing, but Nico's familiarity with the room allowed him to stride halfway across and turn on the lamp near one of the flower-covered tables.

Myrna rolled over to face them, sitting up, confused.

"Nico? What—"

Her brown eyes went wide when she saw Crocetti's currently dismal state.

"Oh my God! What happened? Are you hurt? Where did all that blood come from?" Myrna shrieked.

Nico realized that he wasn't entirely sure. He looked at the other man in the room.

"Benny, whose blood is this all over me?"

"Mickey Clean."

Crocetti turned back to Myrna, repeating flatly, "Mickey Clean."

She ripped the blankets from atop her, casting her legs over the side and standing in one smooth motion. Myrna had no reason to care that she was garbed only in her sleeveless white nightgown with another man in the room—even if it was just Benny.

"No. What happened?" She asked again.

Crocetti sighed. "Arturo Casadonte came at us at the warehouse tonight." He looked at her with a sense of urgency. "You need to get dressed, and we need to go. They could be coming here now."

Myrna gasped, seeing Joey nearly pass by the door and stopping in his tracks when he noticed they were in there.

"No, it's okay, Mrs. Crocetti," Benny said when he realized what had startled her. "It's just Joey."

Her reaction caused a heated sensation in Nico's veins like steam through a pipeline. He had to take a moment to compose himself—return to calm. Crocetti could handle it if guys like Casadonte wanted to send his people to shoot at him, but the thought of his wife being in danger—scared—he wanted to console her, but there was too much blood on his hands.

Joey started to enter the bedroom, but Nico held up a hand, creating an invisible barrier that prevented him from crossing the threshold.

"Joey is going to post outside the door while I get washed up and change clothes, myself," he said to his wife. "Just come out whenever you're ready."

Myrna nodded, still unable to completely wrap her mind around the situation that had roused her from an already uneasy slumber.

Crocetti then left, with Benny in tow, closing the bedroom door. He turned to Joey.

"Stay right here. If anyone comes down that hall, you empty that clip."

Nico then led Benny to his office, withdrawing the key to unlock the door.

"Your nose is looking better," he said.

"It's still a little sore—one side ain't breathing right yet," Benny replied, "But I'm making it work with what I got."

Once they were in the office, Crocetti approached his desk and pulled the telephone to his ear, dialing away on the rotary. Benny stood by idly with his hands in his pockets, glancing toward the door every few seconds.

"Lucetti didn't show," Nico said to the person on the other end of the telephone. "What do you mean? Well, how many guys you got left? All right. We're going to be leaving in less than an hour—just meet me at the usual place. You still got some of those eighteens? Bring them."

Hanging up the phone, Crocetti made his way to the adjoining bedroom he had been using during the months he had made the place a semi-permanent residence.

"Your turn," he said to Benny.

Benny grasped the receiver as Nico went into the bedroom, closing the door behind him.

When he looked into the mirror, even Crocetti was taken aback by his own appearance. His eyes and the area around them were the only features of his face that were recognizable. The rest was covered in a deep crimson hue.

It took a few seconds and a lot of soap to remove the color from his hands, and when the slick cleanser was sufficiently washed away, he filled them with water and washed his face. He didn't bother drying his hands—except for on his pants—and took no care in removing his clothes. They were already ruined, anyway.

Within minutes, Nico was looking like his old self again. Garbed in one of his gray suits with a black tie, he took a moment to comb his hair before donning one of the matching gray hats. He paused before grabbing one of the black ones as well.

Crocetti straightened his collar and secured the knot of his tie, going back into the office to check on Benny.

From the conversation, he could tell that Benny was finishing up a discussion with one of the Gambino brothers. There were three of them: Horatio, Giovanni and Brizio. Their crew was slightly smaller than the one Lucetti ran, and the major difference was that the Gambino brothers always hated Salvadore Barone with a passion. They were the sort that no one wanted to be seen with, because it was common knowledge what they did to eke out a living. The police never bothered with them, however, unless they were caught in the act—Horatio did five years recently—because the cops always wanted to use them as bait to get to the bigger fish. And to most people, that made the Gambino brothers a liability that no one could afford. Nico had kept them afloat over the years because he always believed in having a backup plan in those times when no one else could be counted on to do the right thing.

"That's right," Benny was saying. "The factory on Tenth Street. We should be there in about an hour. Good. We're going to need all three of you."

Benny returned the receiver to the base. "You heard that?"

Crocetti nodded. "Did you get a hold of Lucetti?"

Benny threw his arms up. "Nothing. No answer at the place you've been letting him use to store that hardware."

Maybe Benny had been right earlier. Perhaps they escaped the massacre just in time for Lucetti and his men to show up and get the same treatment.

Nico tossed the black hat to Benny, who turned it over in his hands to give it a good look before putting it on his head. He looked up to Nico with gratitude.

"What are we going to do when we get to the factory?" Benny asked.

"What do you think? First, we're going to put Myrna up in the best hotel close to Twelfth street. Then, we're going to make the only move we got left now. We'll find out whatever we can regarding the whereabouts of Gyp Lucetti and those guns I got for him. After that, it will be time to make funeral arrangements for Arturo Casadonte, Frank Palmer and anyone else on the list."

Crocetti checked to make sure the pistol inside his coat was secure. He turned to Benny once more as they approached the door.

"It's time to put these dogs back on their leashes."

NINETEEN

Friday, April 16, 1937.

IT WAS ALMOST CERTAIN that Nico Crocetti would be dead by now. Palmer absently tapped his wedding band on the top of the steering wheel, lost in thought until he finally reached that realization.

In the hours that followed the call to Arturo, Palmer had second-guessed his decision more than once. He had virtually ordered a mob hit on someone, though his mind attempted to rationalize it by saying he was only giving Casadonte the go-ahead to do something he already wanted to do anyway.

Those concerns were flushed aside with relative ease, however, when he recalled the events that had transpired at his home. The world had shifted overnight, and now there were new rules to play by.

With Crocetti on ice, things would truly be easier now. Arturo would rise to become the city's preeminent businessman, and things would return to a state of relative ease and quietness. Everyone else would fall in line—just like when Barone was calling all the shots.

Something caught his peripheral vision, and Frank looked up. The businessman was wearing the black suit today. Palmer watched as he stepped off the porch of the old white house, getting into his car and backing out the driveway.

That meant it was seven-fifteen.

He didn't want to wake Rose so early in the morning, but after he had explained everything to Donnie's parents, Frank hadn't been able to go back home. For the last four hours, he sat in front of the familiar house contemplating the events of the past several days.

Palmer knew that sleep wouldn't have come easy for him if he had tried to do so. There was too much on his mind. Even though Crocetti was the common denominator, it was Rose Farrell that weighed most heavily on his thoughts.

Once the businessman was out of sight, Palmer started the Ford. It was time to return the car and get some answers in the process.

He was almost sure that his earlier deductions had been correct. It all made sense. Maxwell had likely destroyed that ledger book somewhere along the way.

Maybe something spooked him during the time that they were dipping their hands into Crocetti's pockets, and he decided to get rid of it. Regardless, he was convinced at this point that they were never going to find it. Therefore, it was a non-issue.

And if Crocetti were no longer among the living, then so was that. Once they closed the investigation, word would get around quickly. It always did. The public would learn soon enough that the departed Crocetti was likely involved in the murder of Morgan Maxwell—over gambling debts—and with Crocetti unable to defend himself, it would be pretty easy to shape public opinion from there and make them believe whatever the press wanted them to.

People were gullible that way.

Frank pulled onto one of the lesser-used roads that would take him to the hotel where Rose was staying. He liked having the only car on the road. There was something about the early morning drives that he'd gotten into the habit of taking that put his mind at rest. Perhaps it was because it allowed him to think clearly without any other distractions. After a time, driving becomes mere instinct.

He probably wouldn't tell Callaghan or any of the others what he had deduced. With Crocetti gone, the murder investigation would end. And if Rose did have access to the money that could have been stolen from the mob boss, then there was no point in pursuing it further. He may as well let her keep it and see how far it would get her. But he had to get something, himself—and that something was answers.

Palmer had gone through the conversation many times in his head—anticipating all the ways a guilty woman would go about trying to divert his attention and avoid questions. How she might try to backtrack or only give an answer that wasn't to the question that was asked. It wouldn't be the first time he had to dig into the conscience of a guilty mind and prospect for answers.

The sound of something on the passenger's side ripped him from his thoughts. At first, it was a small humming noise, but that sound intensified until it reached a point to where it sounded like metal scraping across stone. The car kept jerking to the left and Palmer finally decided to pull onto the grass and kill the engine.

He got out and walked around to the other side of the vehicle.

"Damn it."

The front tire was shredded beyond recognition.

He cursed again and walked to the trunk, hoping Rose hadn't lost the tools somewhere along the way.

The trunk was full of loose clothing and what seemed to be a few gifts from past admirers—or fans—if she had ever had such.

Palmer shuffled some of the clothing aside, searching for an iron. The likelihood of there being some oil that would enable him to have an easier time loosening the nuts was a convenience he didn't even bother to ponder.

Finding nothing on one side, he grabbed everything and shifted it to the other. If there were no tools in the trunk, it was going to be a long walk to the nearest telephone.

When Palmer had moved the clothing to the other side, something called for his attention. Among the assortment of women's clothes was a thick black coat that was clearly meant for a man.

Cocking his head to the side, Frank pulled the coat from the trunk. After determining how to turn it in the right direction, he held it high in front of him by the shoulders.

The letter B on the top button gave him every indication.

Bankston Brower.

Palmer quickly laid the coat on the edge of the trunk, running his hands along the brink of the front opening.

One of the buttons was missing.

Frank stepped back, rubbing the scruff of his chin with one hand. Was this Maxwell's coat? If so, why wasn't it in his house with the button when they found him?

Palmer then came to a startling realization. There was only one answer.

Rose Farrell had to have killed Maxwell.

Now it was definitely time to get some answers. Frank shuffled around in the trunk a bit more until he found the tools he needed.

The adrenaline coursing through his body made oil obsolete. After jacking up the car, he removed the nuts with ease. Each one clicked as they tore from the threading.

By the time Palmer had retrieved the spare tire from the side of the car and put it on, there was finally another vehicle approaching in the distance.

"Great timing," he muttered.

As Frank was returning the tools to the trunk, the car slowed as it passed. Traveling down the road a hundred yards, it came to a stop and began to turn around.

Palmer closed the trunk and waved the car off.

"No thanks, pal. All under control here."

Frank was going to pick up the shredded tire from the grass when the car crawled by again. He raised his arm to wave his gratitude for checking on him, but fire burst from the lowered back window.

Palmer instinctively ducked behind the Ford, counting four rounds.

The car sped up again, moving down the road. Frank hurriedly crept around the front of the Ford and jumped into the driver's seat, starting the engine.

The mirror informed him that the other car was turning around to make another pass.

Palmer withdrew Maurice and placed the revolver in the seat beside him, pressing the pedal to the floor. The car lurched from the grass and ejected gravel from the rear.

The other car had already been gathering speed and was coming up fast behind him. Frank took a sharp curve and then saw a straightaway ahead, so he gave the Ford all it had. The needle was pushing near the fifty mark.

Just before he hit fifty miles per hour, the other car hit him from behind. The entirety of the Ford was jostled, and the back end swung out to the side. He twisted the steering wheel in both directions like a madman, struggling to maintain control.

Getting a handling on things again, Palmer sped up as her pursuit persisted. The rural streets of the early morning were clear, and he had the ability to gain plenty of speed without having to avoid any obstacles.

The other car closed on him and began to cozy up to his side. Both windows were down, and he saw two men, each preparing to fire their pistols.

Palmer jerked the wheel hard to the left, smashing the side of the Ford into the other vehicle. Now it was their turn to shimmy and nearly lose control. The driver was a professional, however, and the car only lost a little length, narrowly staying beside him.

As the other car climbed within shooting distance again, Palmer grabbed Maurice and began steering with one hand. He kept glancing to his side while he worked the handle and rolled his own window down.

They were on him again. As soon as the opportunity presented itself, Palmer opened fire. He squeezed off two rounds—one hit the door of the other vehicle, and the other trailed off somewhere into the distance.

The other men returned fire, blowing out the Ford's back window. Another bullet came through the door, just across Palmer's chest.

He slammed the car into the other once again, and both vehicles nearly lost control. They separated as if veering away from one another and Palmer was preparing for them to draw up beside him again when he saw an oncoming vehicle.

The other car was forced to slow and twist back into Palmer's lane behind him. The man in the front passenger's seat continued to fire.

"Damn," Palmer said.

This must have meant that Crocetti was still alive somehow. Usually, when the big roach dies, the others scatter. They wouldn't have been able to reassemble so quickly to come after him again.

Frank was thrown forward as the other vehicle rammed the back bumper again. This time, the bumper came off—thrown underneath the other car.

Palmer didn't think he'd be lucky enough for it to pierce one of their tires.

A bullet hit the back window, causing it to spider web, though it didn't break. He knew it couldn't take another shot before the next ones were coming for his head.

There was another car ahead, traveling in the same direction they were. Palmer watched as the needle was nearly touching sixty, then sixty-five.

The one chasing him was still behind. It had tried to go around him again, but this time, Palmer cut them off, refusing to allow them passage.

Frank prepared himself as the car in front of him drew closer. He would move into the other lane and pass at the last minute, to avoid any oncoming traffic in the curve ahead.

When he felt the time was right, Palmer pulled the wheel to the left, getting ready to make a pass.

But the other car was there.

The two collided and Frank stomped the brakes. There was no way to avoid hitting the car in front of him if he couldn't move into the other lane. The vehicle beside him pushed back, and as the Ford's tires burnt on the road, Palmer had to make a split-second decision. He tried to snatch the wheel so that he could pass the car on the other side—in the grass, but his attackers determined that he should go further.

Caught in the curve with nowhere to go, the Ford leaped off the road, soaring through the air. Frank saw the grassy ground coming toward him fast and the front end of the car blew out in all directions when it hit the ground.

It flipped end-over-end three times before coming to a halt upside-down. Numerous pieces of the Ford were left behind in a trail of carnage as smoke billowed from the underside of the vehicle.

The other car continued along its path without slowing down.

TWENTY

PRONE IN THE BACK SEAT of a moving vehicle, Palmer instinctively rolled onto his side and vomited into the floorboard.

He thought the car had stopped moving, so he pulled himself together and crawled from the wreckage.

The remnants of his black Buick lay behind him, burning in the grassy field. He didn't see any sign of the road.

Frank managed to his feet, feeling a sense of loss as he looked back at his car once again. He scanned the area, but it was trees and grass as far as he could see. So he started walking in the opposite direction from the Buick.

He found a trail that led through the woods and began to follow it until finally, he came upon an enormous tree stump—atop which sat Arturo Casadonte. He was dressed to the nines in his full business attire, smoking a cigarette.

"Things didn't work out like we planned," Arturo said.

He offered Palmer a cigarette. Frank lit it and Arturo motioned for him have a seat on the stump.

"We tried to find her," Arturo continued, "but I give up."

A female voice called out. "That's because I chose the best hiding place ever. But you can't just sit at base and wait for me—that's not how you play. It has to be against the rules somewhere."

Cesca rounded the corner. She was exactly as Frank remembered her two years ago, except that she was wearing the red button-up dress from the movie poster he had seen of *A Simple Moment*, along with white tights. She had a red ribbon in her hair, keeping it up and well secured.

"See," Arturo said. "I told you she had a secret place that I still haven't figured out. I don't think we should play this game with her anymore."

"And it's a good thing it ended when it did," Cesca said. "Because they're looking for you, Frank."

Palmer nodded and removed himself from the stump, continuing to smoke the cigarette as he moved up the trail and back to the orphanage.

When he reached the top of the trail, the old white house stood before him. He flicked the cigarette into the dirt and approached the woman standing on the front porch.

He was expecting Mrs. Ernestine, but it was his mother, instead. She seemed like a giant as she stood there, somehow nearly twice his size in a brown dress and apron. Her blonde curls were styled like the women she had seen in the movies.

"What were you doing?" She asked.

Palmer just stared up at her, not sure exactly what he'd been caught doing this time.

"You know what I mean, Francis Palmer. You were out all night again. But it's not that which I find so frustrating. What concerns me most is—why were you driving so fast?"

There was a great affront to his senses, and Frank sat up. The burning in his nose wouldn't stop. For a minute, he thought he was home and in bed.

"I know it smells bad," a static-filled radio voice said. "But I think you have a concussion. You have to try to stay awake."

Palmer rolled to his side and got out of bed, stumbling his way into Morgan Maxwell's study.

When he entered, Charlie Callaghan was standing near the bookcase with one of the ledger books in his hand.

"Hey, look at this, Palmer," he said.

Callaghan held up what Palmer could only guess was the missing ledger book, revealing the back of the orange cover.

"Right here," Callaghan continued, "it says Salvadore Barone gave you three-thousand dollars."

Maxwell was still lying on the floor, sprawled out in the same position that Palmer remembered him in.

Joe McCreary was standing over Maxwell, holding a fat cigar in one hand. He shook his head as he looked down at the expired radio host.

"It's a shame he had to have such an unfortunate encounter with Mortuary. Ever since Charlie found that other button..."

Another voice appeared from the aether.

"Listen to me, Palmer. You have to stay awake. This is important. I know where Crocetti is. Everything is on Twelfth Street—the guns, Lucetti—everything you need to put Crocetti away."

Jesse Fisher glanced over to Palmer and shrugged. "Don't look at me. It ain't my case. We're just providing support."

"You okay, partner?" Callaghan asked. "You're looking a little green."

Palmer rolled over and vomited in the trash can again. He was able to keep his eyes open, although they rolled back into his head and he almost lost consciousness again at least once.

He could hear music coming from the living room.

Palmer pulled himself from the bed. He was still wearing the same clothes from before, except his jacket had been removed. His tie was severely loosened, and there was a tear in the shoulder of his shirt.

Everything in his body ached, and he had to grab the nightstand to steady himself once he stood. He closed his eyes, covering them with his hand for a minute and then took baby steps toward the living room.

The curtains were blacker than the wall, and they looked like ashes that had somehow managed to barely hold together—the slightest touch and they would fall apart.

He saw that the box on the coffee table had been opened. Photos of Cesca and himself were spread all over the table, including their wedding photo. He checked to make sure he was still wearing his wedding band.

The music ended, and the familiar voice of Morgan Maxwell came on the radio. Frank didn't hear the first part, so it didn't make the punchline funny.

"So that's when I told my wife," Maxwell's radio voice said, "I'd rather have the turkey!"

"You were never married, jackass," Frank replied.

He took a deep breath and sat on the sofa, leaning his head against the back cushion and closing his eyes. He didn't know what time it was, but checking the clock just didn't seem imperative at the moment.

"And that was one of the favorite lines we all remember. So stick around, listeners, and enjoy some of the greatest moments of his career as we continue our week-long tribute to Morgan Maxwell."

An insatiable thirst forced Frank to get back up. He wasn't steady on his feet, but he successfully navigated his way to the kitchen and made a glass of water, which he gulped down in an expedient fashion. He then wished the aspirin wasn't all the way in the bathroom in the medicine cabinet.

Palmer didn't feel like walking that far, so he returned to the sofa and allowed the radio to continue.

They were even playing some of the advertisements Maxwell had lent his voice to. He seemed to have shilled all kinds of products—everything from potholders to vacuum sweepers.

Another unfunny comedy act came up next, and Palmer was beginning to wonder what everyone seemed to think was so special about the guy.

"Just a con artist ripping off gangsters," Palmer muttered.

He opened his eyes and took another look around the living room. From what he had been able to assemble so far, someone had brought him home after the car crash, and he had one indicator of who that most likely was.

If that was the case, then the details about Crocetti and his people being on Twelfth Street wasn't just part of that weird dream.

There was no doubt now that Crocetti was still alive. He survived the hit and then sent a few more goons looking for Palmer. They probably checked his house first and then rode around the area until they found him changing the tire on—

Rose's car. There was no returning it to her now.

Frank rested his head again. There would be time to deal with that once he could actually walk straight.

Maxwell came on the radio again for another shill.

"Hey, you people all know I'm a busy guy, right? With guest spots, public appearances—sometimes my work keeps me away from my work, you know? But it's not all dirt, because with the conveniences of modern technology, sometimes I can almost do the show from home. So, when I know I'm not going to be able to make a live show, I cut the record from my study the night before. And when I do, I only trust one thing, and it's a sure—"

Palmer sat up straight on the sofa with a start.

"Son of a bitch!"

TWENTY-ONE

CALLAGHAN JUST STOOD there, turning his hat in his hands like a steering wheel, looking at Palmer and awaiting an explanation.

"What are you doing here?" Palmer asked. "You found that missing book, right?"

"No," Callaghan said. "I'm here because you called me and told me to come get you. Told me you needed a ride, remember? And where is your car?"

Palmer avoided the question about the car.

"Yeah, that's right. We need to go have a look at something."

"Are you okay? You look awful." Callaghan grabbed Palmer underneath the arm, assisting him in getting to a vertical base.

"Yeah," Palmer said. "I'll be fine."

Callaghan surveyed the photos on the coffee table, pulling the brim of his hat down.

"I didn't know you were married."

"I was," Palmer said. "She died."

"I'm sorry. I had no idea..."

"That's because none of us talk about it."

"Who?" Charlie asked.

"Everyone," Palmer said as he stood up. "Including you and me."

He checked his shoulder holster—Maurice was gone. He didn't know where his hat was, either, but that didn't really matter now.

Palmer donned his coat and kept reaching into his pockets and producing nothing, then patting the outsides of them.

"Where are we going?" Charlie asked.

"Maxwell's." Palmer finally found his keys on the kitchen counter.

"You're not driving, remember? Why are we going to Maxwell's? Did we miss something?"

"Maybe," Palmer said. "I won't know for sure until we have a look."

Once they had gotten into Callaghan's car, the two were quiet for a time. Even through the haze in his brain, Palmer could feel the tension. Gripping the steering wheel tightly, Charlie looked over at Palmer, sighing.

"I'm pretty steamed with you."

Palmer sat with his head in his hand, looking downward and not bothering to move.

"Oh yeah?"

"I don't know what you've been doing the past few days, but I do know that whatever it is hasn't included your partner."

Palmer finally looked up.

"Don't give me that look. You know exactly what I'm talking about. I saw your living room—burnt. And you don't want to tell me what happened to your car, so I vividly imagine the very real possibility that it's in about the same shape or worse."

"Can we do this later?" Palmer asked. "I've got a million jackboots running through my head right now."

The car remained silent until after they pulled into Morgan Maxwell's driveway.

Frank groaned when he saw that Milford Burrows was posted at the door again.

"Hey Charlie," Mil said. "Palmer."

"We need to go in and have another look, Mil," Callaghan replied. "Has anyone else been here?"

"Just other details the last couple days. Before that, the reporters kept showing up. But the Captain has had us rotating shifts to make sure no one messes with anything until whoever figures out what the situation is with Maxwell's estate."

Callaghan nodded.

"It's your case, right? You figure out who killed this guy, yet?" Burrows asked.

"Not yet," Palmer said. "But we're close."

The detectives went inside, and Callaghan closed the door before he finally spoke again. "We are?"

Frank grabbed the handrail to steady himself as they ascended the stairs. He didn't bother to follow up with further details.

Maxwell had been long gone from the place of his final moments in the study, and everything else looked exactly as they had left it.

Palmer covered the bookcase with a wave of the hand.

"We need to look through this again. I know McCreary and Fisher did it before we got here, but I don't think they knew at the time what they were looking for."

"And we do?" Callaghan asked.

Palmer nodded as he began pulling books and paperwork from the shelf.

"Any kind of records that may be here."

"We already did that," Callaghan responded. "Just like you said, Fisher and McCreary went through all the records and paperwork—found the two ledger books and searched every inch of the bookcase for the other."

"I'm not talking about that type of records." Palmer pulled a thin white paper sleeve from the shelf. "Audio records."

Frank removed the record from the sleeve and nestled it onto the machine, switching it on and positioning the needle.

Callaghan continued to search the shelf, finding another.

"You keep finding them, and I'll keep playing them," Palmer said.

Maxwell's voice immediately appeared on the record, thanking listeners for tuning into the show again that particular week. Palmer nudged the needle forward every few seconds until he was convinced that it was a broadcast that Maxwell had indeed recorded from home.

The second album yielded much of the same, and the two continued playing them as Callaghan uncovered more from the bookcase.

"I don't think Crocetti killed Maxwell," Palmer finally admitted.

Charlie stopped looking and turned around.

"What? Then who did, in your expert opinion?"

Palmer couldn't tell whether or not that was a jab. He knew Callaghan was still angry with him for what he perceived to be flying solo.

"I think Maxwell didn't have gambling debt at all. I believe it was an elaborate cover to hide the fact that he and Rose Farrell were ripping off Crocetti."

"You mean you think Maxwell was asking for more money and then tucking it away?"

"Something like that," Palmer said.

"If that's the case, then it sounds like an absolutely good reason to assume Crocetti had Maxwell done away with."

Palmer shook his head. He almost told Callaghan about the coat in Rose's trunk, but something stopped him from spilling the details just yet. He still found it difficult to believe that she could have done it. And if she did, he wanted to know why—because it had to be about more than just money.

Callaghan was about to press the issue when the next record began playing.

"My wife means the operation. And eight o'clock is always half past fourteen."

The detectives looked at each other as they listened.

"What...is that?" Charlie asked.

Palmer shushed him as Maxwell's voice continued speaking. The nonsensical annotations continued for the next ten minutes.

"That's some kind of code," Callaghan said. "At least the instructions to the code, anyway."

They listened to the record until the voice ended. The scratch of the record played for the next two minutes until one last message was uttered.

"Radiosendung 107162 - Die Nacht der Ruhe."

Even Palmer felt the chill traverse his body when he heard the words.

"That's German." Palmer didn't understand it, but he knew enough to be able to recognize the language.

Callaghan looked up at Palmer with the expression of someone who was experiencing the most terrifying moment of their lifetime.

"That says, 'Radio Show' and—whatever the number was—then it says, 'The Night of Rest.'" Callaghan said, his voice shaky.

Palmer still hadn't fully recovered from the realization, either, but the shock gave way to something else, and he felt his nails burrowing into his palm.

"This son of a bitch was using these records and his radio show to transfer messages back and forth between the Germans."

TWENTY-TWO

Saturday, April 17, 1937.

THE CYLINDER ROLLED into position and made the familiar click as Charlie Callaghan flipped it back into the revolver and gave it a spin for good measure.

From the driver's side, Palmer glanced over in disbelief.

"What the hell are you doing?" Palmer asked. "Checking to make sure it's still loaded?

Frank remembered loading his .45 himself, before they ever got into the car. Callaghan couldn't remember whether he had put bullets in his gun or not? If that were the case, now was a hell of a time to be verifying such a negligence.

Callaghan looked at him, unaware of what he had done wrong.

"I'm just making one last inspection," he said. "I've never been in a firefight before."

Palmer shook his head and chambered a round. He didn't like automatics—too much of a chance of jamming—not as reliable as a revolver, and it definitely didn't have the familiar feel of Maurice.

Just the thought of that made him burn internally—such a trusty sidearm lost in the wreckage of a Ford Coupe.

Palmer pulled the door handle and glanced over at Callaghan. "You ready?"

Callaghan shook his head. "No, but I guess we're doing this anyway."

The two got out of the car and joined the group parked behind them. Joe McCreary and Jesse Fisher were there, as well as John Benjamin and three others Palmer didn't recall the names of—at least not off the top of his head.

Frank returned the pistol to his shoulder holster and retrieved his shotgun from the trunk of the Buick. "How are we looking?" Palmer asked the Captain.

"Everything is taken care of," Benjamin said. "If it's what your source says it is, and the guns are here, too, they're all going down."

The group had parked down the block from one of the several factories Crocetti had shut down during the recent economic downturn. From the looks of what he had left, he was almost out of business. But Palmer knew that was only the way it appeared from the outside.

With the hot tip that Mortuary had delivered to him—hopefully accurate—everything would finally be brought to a close before lunch.

There would now be absolutely no way to prove the murder—Palmer had gone by to check on the Ford once Charlie dropped him off at his car when they left Maxwell's place. Apparently the car had been in flames when Mortuary pulled him from the wreckage. The coat—the only evidence that could prove the killer's identity—would not have survived.

But now they had something bigger. Maxwell was working with the Germans, and they had the records to prove it. He was never borrowing money from Crocetti—had no gambling debts—instead, he was getting paid to deliver secret messages from his daily radio show. The ledger books alone wouldn't be enough to connect him to Crocetti, but Crocetti could be tied to the MP18s and the Germans he was buying them from. Not to mention what they were likely to find at Crocetti's office and his home once they had taken him into custody.

The Captain performed a final check, making sure everyone was ready. Fisher had worked in a similar factory before he became a cop, and did his best to describe what he figured the layout might be. Benjamin delivered some last-minute instructions, noting that there would be uniforms positioned around back, and the eight men then converged on the factory.

Checking to make sure everyone was prepared, Benjamin gave him the nod, and McCreary kicked the front door wide open. The group flooded into the building like the reverse of an anthill that had been poked. Weapons drawn, they scanned for the faintest signs of movement.

As soon as they entered, they discovered two armed men standing in the front lobby.

"Don't move!" Benjamin yelled as he leveled his pistol.

The men were startled and nearly brought their shotguns to bear, but the weapons clattered to the floor when they saw how badly they were outnumbered. Two of the other detectives approached and gave them new wrist decorations—one of which was left to guard the two.

Fisher pointed in the direction of the main area, while Palmer was thankful that they didn't have to waste their surprise on those two goons.

"This hall is going to connect to adjoining passages," Fisher said. They would have to clear each of the side hallways as they passed, otherwise someone was likely to get a bullet in the back courtesy of a passing patrol.

The main passage yawned forth until it connected to a large center point of the factory, where the heavy machinery once churned. It was there that the detectives discovered their quarry.

Palmer barely had time to notice everyone who was there before they had their weapons drawn. Benjamin wasn't able to shout any orders, either, before the bullets began flying.

The room was filled with crates stacked at various heights. It provided ample cover for both sides and Palmer wasted no time throwing himself behind one of them as the lid of the top container was blown off and hurled through the air, landing in front of him.

Frank knew that he saw the big fish, as well as Benny Cassano, Joey Donati and Gyp Lucetti. He was pretty sure the three Gambino brothers were with them, and he recognized two of Lucetti's men. He wasn't sure who the other four were.

Callaghan was positioned across from Palmer, having yet to have fired off a shot. He pointed to the group with Crocetti.

"I saw them," Callaghan yelled. "Those are the Germans who have been bringing in the guns."

Palmer looked again. Charlie had to be right. If Crocetti and Lucetti's men were all accounted for—plus the three Gambinos—that had to be the Germans.

Taking a quick breath, Palmer pumped the shotgun and twisted upward to release the fire. This caused the rest of his group to follow in fashion.

Sensing the moment, Callaghan had a clear shot at moving forward. Charlie slid behind one of the stacks of crates closer to the opposing group and paused a second before rising and firing over the top.

"What about the back?" Palmer yelled to Benjamin.

"I said it was covered. Ten uniforms back there. These guys aren't going anywhere."

TWENTY-THREE

WHEN THE SHOOTING started, Benny had managed to pull Nico beside him, well covered by one of the crates—for as long as it held up. Crocetti was sitting on the floor with his pistol in his hand, although Benny had no intentions of letting him use it.

Benny turned to Joey, who was a few crates down. The skinnier of the two partners was sitting on the floor, cursing under his breath and fumbling to jam five more rounds into his revolver.

"You always wanted to shoot your way in or out of somewhere," Benny said. "Now's your chance, Two Stacks."

So far, they had been successful in keeping Crocetti from again being covered in blood—his own or otherwise.

The Germans were holding their own, but Benny wished there had been time to obtain some of those automatic weapons from the crates instead of having to use pistols.

Joey squeezed off a few rounds and squatted back down.

"One of the Gambinos is dead," he reported gravely.

Benny stood and took some shots, hitting one of the detectives in the shoulder and whirling him around before landing behind cover.

Nico looked up to Benny. "This is it." He said. "This has to be where we draw the line. And I'm not going to prison."

"And I ain't going back," Benny added.

Gyp Lucetti scrambled over to them. He was panting as if he had just run a mile. Blood stained his vest, but Benny didn't think it looked like he had been hit.

Lucetti was thankful that the problems had been cleared up with Crocetti, having explained the situation that arose with Mortuary. But now he didn't know if it would do any of them any good.

Nico looked at Lucetti. "Is that Frank Palmer?"

"Yes," Lucetti said. "He appears to still be alive."

"I've had enough of that son of a bitch," Crocetti said. His nails slowly dug into his palms with the methodical precision reserved for torture devices.

It wasn't going to end like this. Nico could not allow Myrna to be left alone—no one to care for her; no one to take care of her. Palmer wasn't going to take away what little remained after his brother-in-law's betrayal.

A shotgun blast ripped through one of the nearby crates, causing Joey to lose his footing. He dropped to the floor for a moment, where he took the time to empty the cylinder again.

"Enough of this," Crocetti said. "He wants me."

Benny straightened his hat, eyes peering through the black powder that darkened one side of his face. "You ain't giving up?"

"No," Nico said. "Wherever I go, Palmer is sure to follow."

Lucetti agreed. "I'll get word to my men and the Heinies."

Lucetti then shuffled back toward what was left of his men, taking care to remain crouched low like a cat in unfamiliar territory.

* * * * *

Palmer almost didn't make it as he dove behind closer cover. Everything in his body still ached, and he only moved at just over half his normal speed. Just running was painful enough, but the landing he took mostly on his arms didn't do any favors for the aching stiffness in his shoulders and neck.

Frank looked over the top of the crate just in time to see Crocetti abandoning the fray and moving toward one of the other corridors. Crocetti kept his head down, though he was clearly still armed.

"You see that?" Callaghan called to Palmer.

"Tell them to lay down cover," Frank said.

"What are you doing?" Callaghan asked.

"I'm going after him," Palmer said, discarding the empty shotgun and pulling his .45 from the interior of his coat.

Before Callaghan could protest, Frank was on the move. Charlie had to quickly give the signal to the others. The rest of the detectives began shooting at once, keeping the opposition pinned down while Palmer made his move.

Frank navigated through the crate stacked area of the factory, pausing to put a bullet into the chest of one of Lucetti's men who had spotted him.

He finally broke away, and Palmer knew he was hot on Crocetti's heels.

Avoiding any stupid mistakes, Palmer pushed his back against the wall and peered around the corner before following.

Crocetti had tried to have him killed more than once. He somehow managed to survive the hit Arturo put on him, and he wasn't getting away this time.

The passage led to a larger room where some of the old factory machinery still remained. Palmer carefully entered, bending his knees so that he could keep low, but still move quickly if he had to.

Scarce light penetrated the room from the outside, only offering a sampling of luminance through the small rectangular windows that must have been fifteen feet high on the walls, and the scent of dust and mildew was prominent in the humid atmosphere.

Frank stopped in his tracks when he heard the sound of metal upon metal. The sound echoed throughout the room so that it was impossible for him to tell which direction the sound was coming from.

And then it was there.

Palmer ducked backward, arching his back so that he quickly threw himself on his side. Pain shot through his ribs, but he glanced up to see that he had narrowly avoided a giant hook connected to a chain—used to lift heavy machinery—that had been launched in his direction, gliding to a stop hear the doorway he had entered.

Palmer scampered to a steel girder nearby before standing upright again and regaining his composure.

"I know you're in here, Crocetti," Palmer called into the darkness. He slowly raised his weapon in preparation.

The last response Frank had expected to hear was the sound of laughter.

Palmer peered into the shadow from the outer edge of the girder, moving around it like a gravitational orbit until he pulled away and jogged to the next closest girder he could see.

He couldn't see anything else. The deeper Palmer got within the storage room, the darker it became. The light from the entrance was no longer a factor.

Twisting to take another look, Palmer was unprepared for what came from the other direction. Nico Crocetti pounced from the darkness, brandishing a large knife that reminded Frank that there was no sting like the bite of cold steel.

His coat took the brunt of the weapon, but Palmer knew that his shoulder had been sliced open, and the sleeve began to warm almost immediately.

Frank bounced backward on his toes just in time to avoid a wide arc that was intended to split him left to right.

Nico still wore a smirk.

"Something funny?" Palmer asked.

"It's going to be funny for a long time to come, I think."

"What's that?"

"You," Nico said. "And everything you think you represent."

"Sounds like German spy talk to me," Palmer said flatly, unlooping his necktie and jerking it through his collar so that he could wrap each end around one of his hands.

Crocetti came at him again, but he was close enough that instinct forced Palmer to give him a left jab in the cheek. It was enough to knock the older man back, disorienting him for a moment

Palmer leapt at the opportunity, wrapping his necktie around the arm Crocetti wielded the knife with. Crocetti punched Frank in the back of the head with his free hand, frantically attempting to drive the blade into Palmer's chest with the other.

Frank ducked low, then pushed himself off his feet with all the strength in his legs. He drove his shoulder into the bottom of Crocetti's chin, and Palmer heard the sound of teeth breaking from close proximity.

His hands became increasingly wet, and Palmer stepped back to find that the knife was stuck deep in Crocetti's abdomen, reminding him of a toothpick in the top of a sandwich at a fancy dinner party.

Crocetti sank to his knees. He looked up at Palmer, and when he spoke, his broken teeth empowered him to spit crimson defiance.

"Do you really believe I'm all there is?" Crocetti asked. "I'm not the head of this snake, and I'm not the tip of the iceberg either."

Nico pulled the knife from his body, and it tumbled to the cold floor. Frank's eyes had adjusted to the darkness enough that he could see Crocetti's hands, tethered to his body by scarlet webbing.

Crocetti shook his head. "People like you—you have no idea. Look what has happened to us. What's happened as a country. It's all fallen apart."

"It may be in the toilet right now," Palmer said. "But it's still my favorite toilet."

"Rampant unemployment. Riots. Strikes. A new way needs to be paved. Do you think this will stop us from doing our work? That we will stop coming? We are already here. This society hangs by a thread, and all it needs is one more little push before it collapses. People have lost faith in the government's ability to provide stability. And that government now only serves itself. We will continue to our silent work from within—to give them a new faith—a new world built upon the rubble of this one."

Palmer kept his arm close to his body, reaching down to pick up his pistol with his good hand. "We've got the guns, Crocetti. The Germans, too. We also found everything you wanted from Maxwell's."

"And what was that?" Crocetti asked, slowly reaching behind his back. He lifted his coat, hand itching to grasp the pistol tucked into his slacks.

"The reason you wanted the actress," Palmer stated. "So you could make her go in and get the records. Maxwell's former gal would have been able to do it without arousing much suspicion."

"You think you're so clever," Nico hissed. "But pardon me if I still choose to laugh. I'll use every resource at my disposal to fight a conviction. If I am in prison, I'll utilize my vast resources and still get my messages to my allies. No matter where I am, I will still be running my part of this operation. And in the unlikely event I am in a cell when this is all over, I'll still find my humor. And I'll be thinking of people like you, and how inconsequential you truly are."

Crocetti suddenly snatched the pistol from behind him, bringing it to bear.

Palmer gave no hesitation. He pulled the trigger. Before Crocetti could fire off a shot, Frank put a bullet directly through the mobster's right eye. Crocetti finally stopped talking and collapsed to the floor.

Palmer wondered if he could still run his little operation from the warm confines of hell.

TWENTY-FOUR

Sunday, April 18, 1937.

SHE LOOKED AT HIM with the wide eyes of a woman who knew she had been discovered. Rose Farrell had remained silent the entire time Palmer explained his theory to her, save for the tears that now stained her soft features.

"And with that knowledge of his activities with the Germans, I'm pretty sure you were using it to blackmail him," Frank said at last.

"No," Rose protested, sitting up straight in the chair. "Well, most of what you say is correct, but it's more the other way around."

"How so?" Frank asked.

"I always had a key to his house," she said. "About three months ago, I was going to surprise him, but I walked in on one of his meetings. He and the other man were speaking German."

"Probably one of the ones we arrested yesterday," Palmer said. "Go ahead."

"Morgan swore that if I said anything that the men would find me and make me disappear. So, of course, I stayed quiet about the matter. I didn't know why it was such a secret until later."

Callaghan entered the interrogation room. It was the same one they had used before, and Rose was growing familiar with the arrangements.

"Call *The Amendment*?" Palmer asked.

"Yeah," Callaghan said. "At least now they have a big story that can be halfway believable."

Charlie maneuvered to the empty chair, taking a seat beside Palmer.

Frank made an inviting hand gesture to Rose.

"Continue."

"I was snooping around his study one day while he was at work, trying to find out if he was in danger—and if so, how much. But then I found one of the records still on the cutting machine—it was one of those with the instructions."

"That was all you needed to know, huh?" Callaghan surmised.

"I suspected, but—was he really a complete spy for the Germans?"

Palmer nodded in the affirmative.

"He played a major role, let's just say that," Frank answered. "So, you found one of the records. What did you do then?"

"I waited for him to come home from work. And then I confronted him. I told him that whatever he was involved in, he just needed to get away—say he wasn't doing it anymore, no matter how much they were paying him."

"What did he think about that?" Callaghan asked.

Rose wiped her eye again with the back of her hand.

"He said that no one was making him do it. That he had been talking to these people for a long time, and he believed in them—what he was doing was going to save the country from complete ruin."

"There's a difference of opinion there," Callaghan remarked, glancing over to Palmer.

"So, what then?" Palmer asked.

"Well," she said, "That was when we stopped seeing each other regularly. But he had to make sure to keep a watch on me, so he continued paying for my apartment. Every couple weeks he would come by with flowers and ask me a hundred questions about what I knew and who I had told."

"Let's get to the part where you killed him," Callaghan said.

Frank looked over at Charlie. He was almost proud to see that the rookie's small battle-test had made him see things now with a new pair of eyes. The naiveté was fading.

"I went to his house," she recalled. "It was raining, and I was soaked. "When I went inside, I shed most of my wet clothing, and he put his coat around me. He took me up to his study, and I told him that I thought what he was doing was wrong. I said that if he didn't stop immediately, that I was going to go to the police."

"That set him off?" Palmer asked.

Rose shifted in her chair. She swallowed hard before she continued.

"He had a gun—I'd never seen one before. It was frightening. Then, he threatened me with it and said that he should...kill me right there. Morgan threw me over the desk and put it to the back of my head."

Now it was Palmer's turn to find discomfort in his chair, so he stood up instead.

"I started crying," she said. "He pulled me back up and then said he could throw me through the window instead. I tried to fight back—I think I grabbed the gun—and it went off. It startled us both, but then I realized that I was the one who had the gun. He came at me and without thinking, I did what I could to defend myself."

"The gun—you put it in the coat pocket and got out of there as fast as you could," Palmer concluded.

Rose nodded, wiping her eyes again.

"What did you do with the gun after that?" Callaghan asked.

"I drove outside the city and tossed it in a lake."

Palmer nodded, placing his hands on the back of the chair. It could be argued as self-defense, but things were going to get muddy once the Feds arrived tomorrow and began to look into things. The murder investigation would probably stay local, but Rose was definitely going to be questioned regarding matters of treasonous espionage on the part of her late flame.

"Well," Frank said, "Are you ready?"

Rose put her sunglasses on, covering the reddening of her eyes. She breathed deeply before straining the hem of her dress and standing up.

"I think so."

Once Crocetti had been put down, the rest of the group had given up without any more bloodshed. Two of the three surviving Gambino brothers, Gyp Lucetti and his men and Benny Cassano and Joey Donati—all taken into custody. Only one of the Germans survived, but so far he wasn't saying a thing.

One of the detectives had taken a hit, but it looked like he was going to pull through. Joe McCreary's face was cut up pretty badly from crate fragments being blown into is face—he wasn't expected to miss any time on the job.

Roselyn Farrell was the only loose end that remained.

Palmer was slightly taken aback when she slipped her arm into his elbow as if he were a less-than-official escort.

Callaghan opened the interrogation room door, motioning for them to walk through. Then, he joined them on Rose's other side.

The trio caught stares from everyone they passed. Some of the officers shook their head while others looked on in awe.

When they rounded the corner, there were reporters on the other side of the glass doors, in front of the precinct for as far as the eye could see. They became restless when they saw Rose Farrell striding toward them.

The cacophony they created grew louder the closer they got, and when Palmer was sure no one—not even Callaghan—would overhear, he leaned in close to her.

"Good job," he said confidently.

She had remembered her lines just as he had instructed and the way the two had played it out while Callaghan was making the call to the newspaper.

They were assaulted by the press when the doors finally opened. Escorted by uniformed officers already waiting out front, Palmer and Callaghan helped them to maintain order as Rose passed through the crowd.

"Miss Farrell! Miss Farrell! Is it true you exposed a German spy ring?"

"Do you know if it has any connection with the Nazis?"

"How did you first learn of Morgan Maxwell's involvement?"

"Is it true that he tried to kill you?"

"They're already discussing a movie. Will you be playing yourself?"

Palmer had pulled some strings with the Captain, convincing his old partner that even exposing Crocetti and Maxwell didn't solve Maxwell's murder. And considering the way that it happened, if they were already going to tarnish the celebrity status of Morgan Maxwell, then what they needed was a hero—or in this case, a heroine—on the other side.

It didn't change the fact that Roselyn Farrell killed Morgan Maxwell. The grand jury would still have to convene, but they weren't holding her on any charges, and it was almost certain she wouldn't be brought to trial— even Palmer would verify the validity of the self-defense claim. And Callaghan's discovery of the bullet in the floor would help to back that up.

Rose had been credited with uncovering the entire link between Maxwell, the Germans and Crocetti and exposing it to the police. The only thing that was conveniently left out was that she hid the knowledge of Maxwell's death, but Palmer felt no guilt over leaving out some of the details, himself.

"Miss Farrell! Are you going back to Hollywood?"

"Are you still signed with a studio?"

"How does it feel to be a role model for women everywhere?"

Roselyn smiled as Palmer opened the cab for her. Climbing into the back seat, she lowered her sunglasses and thanked him with her eyes before he gave her the nod and closed the door. The blonde continued to stare at him in wonderment over the top of her glasses until he turned around.

Then, with Callaghan's assistance, Frank helped the uniformed officers block the reporters while the taxi was cleared to make its getaway.

TWENTY-FIVE

Monday, April 19, 1937.

WHEN SEVEN-FIFTEEN arrived the next morning, Frank was parked in his usual spot, down the street from the white old house. Dark clouds gathered in the morning sky, but the speed in which they moved gave Palmer feeling that if it were going to storm, it would pass through quickly.

The car was still in the driveway of the white house, but the businessman had not yet made an appearance. He was running late.

Frank wondered if he was now one of the unemployed.

He lit another cigarette and for the first time in a while, he felt content.

Arturo would now be able to run his empire unimpeded, and Rose Farrell was—at least temporarily—the most famous woman in America.

Best of all, no one was trying to kill him anymore.

The businessman finally presented himself about ten after eight. He was wearing a white short-sleeve shirt and what appeared to be his pajama pants. Descending the front steps, he carried a sign underneath his arm, which he stuck in the ground once he had made it near the curb.

Taking a closer look, Palmer narrowed his eyes and realized that the sign was on a white background and the words 'For Sale' were written in bold red lettering.

Frank cocked his head and stepped out of the car. He had gotten used to seeing the businessman on many mornings when he was lost in thought, but he had never even met the man, nor did he have any clue as to what his name was.

The businessman straightened the sign and stepped back to take a look at it before straightening it again.

"Good morning," Palmer said as he approached, pushing his hands into his coat pockets.

The man idly waved, almost lost in giving the sign a third inspection.

"Morning."

Palmer gestured to the sign, stating the obvious but making conversation anyway.

"Moving out?" Frank asked.

"Yeah," the man said. "Got a transfer up to Boston, so I decided to take it. With the way things are here, I figured there would be more opportunity for advancement there."

Frank kicked the signpost with the toe of his shoe. "You got a buyer yet?"

"I just now put the sign up."

Palmer felt little guilt in waiting until after the businessman was satisfied with his arrangement before informing him that he was going to have to take it back up.

"No need to keep it," Palmer said. "I think I'm going to buy the place."

The man laughed at Frank's impulsiveness. "Don't you at least want to see the inside first?"

"I already know what it looks like," Palmer said.

Frank turned his head to look up at the ivory monolith casting a morning shadow over the lawn, stretching all the way to the road. The front porch was westward-facing, which would allow for some relaxing coffee and cigarette mornings without the sun in his eyes.

"I grew up in that house."

The businessman cocked his head back, making a surprised guttural sound. "Nathan Palmer was your old man?"

"Why?" Frank asked. "Did you know him?"

"No, but when we moved in there was an old box of the family's things in the loft—photos and a few medals and such. We didn't have the heart to throw it away, so we just left it there along with the things we put up there. I can dig it out for you if you want to come by and pick it up later."

"That's okay," Palmer said. "Just leave it in the attic for me when you move out."

It was another box of memories he'd have to leave packed away. He knew, though, that he would have to go through it at least once. He barely remembered what his parents looked like anymore.

"I never expected it would sell so quickly," the businessman said, extending his hand. "Jack Reynolds."

Frank took his hand in kind, introducing himself.

"Frank Palmer?" Jack asked. "You're the detective from the papers, right? My wife loves Roselyn Farrell—she's her favorite actress of all time."

Palmer wondered how new that revelation was for Jack's wife.

They exchanged small talk for awhile, discussing everything from what Palmer felt like revealing about the case to the neighborhood and how it hadn't changed much in the time that the Reynolds family had been there. Jack also explained a few of the minor problems that probably needed to be fixed in the house. He noted that the pipes sometimes creaked at night, but he couldn't figure out what it was. And there was a spot around back where he thought the mice were getting in. If it were repaired before winter, though, that would do wonders in keeping them out.

When they were finished with the conversation, they finally agreed on a date and time to meet at the bank. Palmer informed Reynolds that he would be able to pay in cash.

Shaking hands once again, Palmer bid Jack Reynolds farewell and opened the car door before taking another long look at the house.

It was going to be his again.

Then, he climbed into the Buick and headed home.

Palmer was tempted to avoid the back roads after what happened the other morning, but he didn't believe in lightning striking twice.

Besides, there probably wasn't anyone around who wanted to run him off the road.

He wasn't Roselyn Farrell, but his involvement in the case was probably going to gain him a level of local fame.

He didn't want it.

When he was on the God's Acre Murders two years ago, he would have still let his retiring partner have all the spotlight anyway—even if his wife hadn't been taken from him in the middle of the case.

Frank had saved up enough money—combined with what Salvadore Barone left him—to buy the house with plenty to spare.

Maybe it was time to start seriously thinking about leaving the force and going into business for himself. As a private investigator, just like he had told Casadonte.

When Palmer pulled into his driveway, he noticed a man sitting on his front porch. The stranger was dressed in regular clothing—a tieless shirt and brown pants. He was tall and lean, and his stance led Palmer to believe that he was either a little nervous, impatient or both.

At his side was a wooden crate about three feet tall, with a much smaller one stacked on top of it.

Palmer closed the car door, dropping the keys into his pocket.

"Can I help you?" Palmer asked.

"You Frank Palmer?"

He regarded the man's attire again.

"You don't look like the postman," Frank said.

"No, I'm not. And if you ain't Detective Frank Palmer, then this ain't for you."

Frank drew his coat to the side, allowing the light of the morning sun to gleam from the surface of his badge.

The man bobbed his head when he saw it, appearing suitably convinced.

"Sorry, but I had to be sure," he said. "A guy paid me to bring these things here personally. Told me to wait for you if you weren't home."

"What guy?"

"He didn't say his name," the freelance delivery man stated.

Palmer was already tired of playing the guessing game. "Well, what did he look like?"

"He was tall—not as tall as you—probably about five years older than you, though. How old are you—about forty? Yeah, definitely older than you."

Palmer was thirty-two. He knew it had been a rough week or so, but he didn't think it had put eight years on him.

"What else?" Frank asked.

The delivery man shrugged, "And he had dark hair. Look, he gave me a hundred bucks to do it, so I didn't ask too many questions."

Frank put his hand on the larger box, inspecting it for a moment before looking back to the delivery man.

"And that's all you know?" Palmer asked.

"That's all I know, sir."

"All right, then. You take the big one."

Palmer grabbed the small box with one hand and unlocked the front door. He was already going to be moving boxes again soon, and he didn't want to experience that misery until that moment was truly at hand. Plus, his neck was worse today than it had been previously—he wondered if he'd be able to even turn it once the day was over.

Frank did, however, give the delivery man the courtesy of holding the door open for him when he staggered inside with the wooden crate.

"Just put it over by the coffee table," Frank said.

When he was finished, the delivery man dusted his hands as if he'd just completed a job well done, and stood there with his hands in his pockets, looking at Palmer.

He had to be joking.

"You want a tip?" Palmer asked. "I don't even know what's in that thing. Could be money. Could be a body."

"Nah," the delivery man argued. "Wasn't heavy enough for a body. Well, maybe enough for a medium-sized dog, I guess."

Palmer sighed and pulled his money clip from his pocket. He didn't think a mystery prize was worth as much as keeping his house from burning down, but he peeled off a five-dollar bill and handed it to the man anyway.

When he had finally gotten rid of the delivery man, Palmer sighed, looking at the coffee table. The photos were still there, along with the empty box, so he tucked them neatly back into place with the scarves that had kept the memories warm.

As far as the most recent boxes were concerned, he could get the small one open with his knife, but he had to find his pry bar to be able to handle the big one.

Inside the smaller box was a miniature record—unmarked and not very different from the ones he and Callaghan had found at Maxwell's.

Palmer held the record up to inspect it before he put it on the player and touched the needle to the surface. The beginning scratch went on for around ten seconds before it finally gave way to a voice.

"Hello, Detective Palmer."

It was a man's voice. Frank didn't recognize it, but whoever he was knew his name.

"You said you never wanted to be the man who caught Mortuary, but it is my sincere hope that you will still find him, no matter how much you strive to avoid it. You see, he's inside me, and he's inside you."

It had to be him.

Frank's gaze fell upon the larger box that he had left the pry bar atop.

Palmer tore the box open, looming above to get a clear look into its three-feet depth.

On the top was a black cloth material. He pulled it from its tucked position and discovered the soulless black eyes of Mortuary.

"I will do you the courtesy of explaining the contents you shall find within."

The black mask gazed up at him, searching for the darkness inside that it had referenced on the rooftop.

Palmer was hesitant to pick it up. He reached down and drew his hand back before finally taking it. The mask felt cold in his hands—it wasn't metal, and it wasn't hardened rubber—he didn't know what it was composed of.

"The mask is hinged to a skullcap that will protect all sides of your head. Inside the mouth is a microphone that will distort your voice and render it unrecognizable. The lenses are built to amplify ambient light, which should remedy your night-blindness. Additionally, the filter within the mask will compensate for airborne toxins or even smoke."

Beneath the mask was a pair of folded metal frames. There was a larger circular-shaped ring on the top and a smaller one on the bottom, connected by long pieces on each side.

"The braces are composed of an alloy with springs in the knees and ankles that work similar to shock absorbers on an automobile. They will allow you to land from great heights, but you will still need to roll with the fall. They have thus far been tested up to approximately sixty feet."

Those items had been lying atop a black coat and matching clothing that Palmer only guessed would have been what was worn underneath.

"The jacket and interior suit are lined with an alloy mesh that can stop most handguns—though it is still an

uncomfortable experience. It is not recommended that you test it against rifles. I took the liberty of replacing the coat button for you."

Palmer gathered the assortment that was on top, extracting them from the box to get to the coat. It was surprisingly light to have been something that was said to be lined with a metal weave.

"The same alloy is sheathed within the gloves—most notably in the knuckles—allowing for a punch to be delivered with the impact of a heavyweight boxer. The padding underneath also protects your hands from being broken in the process."

Below the enhanced clothing articles, Palmer discovered matching boots and three weapons.

"There is nothing noteworthy about the boots. And you know what to do with a pair of Colt 1911 pistols. I also retrieved something of yours from the wreckage that morning."

Palmer's mouth curled into a grin when he saw Maurice lying in the bottom of the box, curled up comfortably between the two .45s. He had already been convinced he would never again feel that familiar grip in his hand.

Palmer thumbed the cylinder open and emptied the combination of bullets and empty casings into his hand, laying them on the table where they rolled around in different directions until one of them fell over the edge.

Frank relaxed his large frame onto the sofa, contemplating the items gathered around him on the floor.

The recording continued, but the sound became distorted and vitiated, changing to the distinct voice Palmer recognized as being that of Mortuary.

"First, there was God's Acre; then there was Rohde Falls. In time, you are sure to meet another devil that eclipses radiance from the world. It is for this day that I have given you the tools to enter the shadows and resuscitate the heartbeat of a dying light."

Frank laid the revolver gently on the coffee table and again turned his attention to the pile of clothing on the floor.

"For if in you—as I have long suspected—there exists a resolute ferocity to be wrought against the wicked... It was meant to be seen."

As Palmer leaned back on the sofa, he noticed that half of the mask was peeking from underneath the black clothing on the floor.

And it was still looking at him.

ABOUT THE AUTHOR

WYATT HAMBY was born and educated in Georgia. After serving in the US military, he has spent over a decade as a technical author and instructional designer in a variety of mechanical and petroleum engineering fields, where his work has become the standard for a number of global companies. He currently resides in Houston, Texas.